**She didn't care what people
in Prospect thought of her.**

But she did, she reminded herself. These people might hold the key to finding Joshua, and that was the best reason of all.

And a little corner of her mind niggled at her: *You care what Ben thinks.*

Mariah straightened her back and firmed her resolve. She didn't care about the people in Prospect, she didn't care about her appearance, and she certainly didn't care about Ben.

So there, she said to her reflected image. *Now go into town and find Joshua. The sooner you can do that, the sooner you'll be out of this dusty place and back in the cradle of civilization.*

And away from Ben? the little voice persisted.

She ignored it. Yes, she ignored it.

JANET SPAETH

In first grade, Janet Spaeth was asked to write a summary of a story about a family making maple syrup. She wrote all during class, through morning recess, lunch, and afternoon recess, and asked to stay after school. When the teacher pointed out that a summary was supposed to be shorter than the original story, Janet explained that she didn't feel the readers knew the characters well enough, so she was expanding on what was in the first-grade reader. Thus a writer was born. She lives in the Midwest and loves to travel, but to her, the happiest word in the English language is *home*.

Books by Janet Spaeth

HEARTSONG PRESENTS

The Lilac Year

Janet Spaeth

Heartsong Presents

He that goeth forth and weepeth, bearing precious seed,
shall doubtless come again with rejoicing,
bringing his sheaves with him.
—Psalm 126:6

A note from the Author:

I love to hear from my readers! You may correspond with me by writing:

Janet Spaeth
Author Relations
P.O. Box 9048
Buffalo, NY 14240-9048

ISBN-13: 978-0-373-48631-1

THE LILAC YEAR

This edition issued by special arrangement with Barbour Publishing, Inc., 1810 Barbour Drive, Uhrichsville, Ohio, U.S.A.

Prologue

January 17, 1887
The Dakota Territory

The little boy stood in front of the platform at the Grange Hall. The air was close and stale, and faces swam in front of him until he felt dizzy.

Mrs. Soames had told him that he had a very special home waiting for him in the West. When he'd asked if his mother would be there, the kind woman had shaken her head sadly and explained it all over again: that his mother had a new home, too, but hers was in heaven.

Heaven. He'd heard of it, so many times, as Mama told him stories from the big book with the black leather cover. Wonderful stories they were, too—tales

of a man named Noah and a fellow called Jonah and
that sweet woman Ruth.

But best of all were the stories of Jesus. Once
Mama told him that Jesus had said He went to heaven
to make a home for everyone. One day they would be
there, and Jesus would be there, and there would be
nothing but happiness.

A tear caught in his eyelashes, and he tried to will
it away. He did not want anyone to see it. Crying was
for babies, and he was not a baby.

He held his breath and thought about Jonah and
what the inside of a whale's belly must look like, or
even worse, smell like.

The inside of the Grange Hall wasn't nearly as bad
as that. It didn't smell great—stuffy with scents like
pipes and men and smoke from the black-crusted stove
that heated the building in the winter—but he was sure
it smelled better than a whale's stomach.

"Joshua Carleton Brighton!"

At the sound of his name, the boy stepped forward
and stared at the back of the auditorium. He didn't want
to look too eager, like Zena and Tommie. They were
on their third trip west.

Those two were at the difficult age, the other children had told him on the train. Too old to be cute and
too young to be much help on a farm.

When Joshua'd asked what that meant, the older
ones had patted him on the head and told him not to
worry: he was still as sweet as a little yellow buttercup.
Joshua didn't believe them. He knew his teeth were

too big for his face, and Mrs. Soames hadn't gotten his hair cut quite evenly.

But he'd be brave. He straightened his shoulders and gritted back the pain in his stomach.

Gradually the faces came into focus, and Joshua could see their eyes on him. A couple in the front row looked him over speculatively from their chairs. Joshua thought he saw the woman's eyes soften, but the man beside her leaned over and whispered something in her ear. Joshua knew what he'd said: "Too little."

He looked farther into the audience. He saw a woman with a flat, firm mouth, not at all gentle and smiling like his mother's, and he quickly looked away.

To her left another man and woman stared at him. The woman chewed on her lip a moment before shaking her head no.

Everywhere he looked, he saw rejection, and he knew he was going to be like Zena and Tommie. No one would want him—ever.

And then what would happen to him? What happened to the children who were not chosen? It was a question he didn't dare ask.

"You've seen them," Mr. Soames said to the crowd. He and Mrs. Soames had taken the group all the way out here, and pretty soon, he'd heard the man say to his wife, they'd reach the end of the line for this trip. "Look at their eyes. Right now, they're clear and pure. But give them a month on the streets, and they'll be hawking papers and smoking cigarettes. These tender little hands will soon be raw and chapped. The worst part of those who live this sad life on the streets of New

York City is the haunted and lost look in their eyes. Each child, every single one of them, sees the same future, the same bleakness."

Mr. Soames paused and slowly wheeled around, pointing to each person gathered there. "You can save them. Can you open your heart? Your home? Your life? Can you save one of these precious ones?"

Joshua's eyes grew hot and itchy, and he wanted to rub them, but he didn't dare. Someone might think he was crying, and he was too old for that. Nobody would want a boy who cried.

It wasn't supposed to be like this, he told himself. In the storybooks his mother had read to him, everything turned out happily ever after. He didn't see any chance of that here.

He felt a touch on his sleeve, and he turned. The eyes he looked into were caring and friendly, and the smile he received was encouraging. Maybe he had found a home at last. Maybe there was a happily ever after.

"How old are you, son?"

Chapter 1

June 16, 1887
New York City

"My nephew," Mariah explained again to the man at the desk. "Joshua Brighton."

The man shook his head, and his tiny wire-rimmed glasses bobbled on his nose. "I'm sorry, miss. We can't give you that information. Let me assure you, the boy has been placed in a fine home."

"But he has a home, with me." Mariah drew a deep breath. "Look, I've come all the way from Massachusetts to see my sister and her son, only to find out that she's dead and he's disappeared into your hands. He's only five years old! This day has been excruciatingly difficult already. Please, just tell me this one thing. Tell me where he is!"

"Again, my apologies for your distress. But the young man has been adopted into a good household."

"He's *my* nephew." Mariah's temper flared as red as her hair. "Doesn't that count for anything with you? Why won't you tell me where he is?"

None of this day seemed real. Any moment, she'd wake up and discover it had all been a horrible, horrible dream.

Lorna. Dead. It was unimaginable.

As if that weren't bad enough, she'd also discovered that her nephew, Lorna's son, had been taken by this organization, Orphans and Foundlings. She had walked for miles and asked countless passersby how to get to the agency in the hope of finding Joshua. Now this man—this pompous *toad* of a clerk—seemed determined to block her way.

He lifted his shoulders and dropped them helplessly. "As I said before, once a placement is made, those records are sealed. Perhaps I could interest you in taking another child?"

"I don't want another child! I want my nephew!" Anger and frustration rose in her throat like hot bile. She leaned over the counter and swept the papers off the man's desk, grabbing one and crumpling it in his face. "Why won't you listen to me?"

"Is there a problem?" A large man emerged from the back of the room, where he had been bent over a heavy wooden desk littered with files, and walked around the counter to Mariah. "I'm Jack Stone," he said, extending a fleshy hand toward her.

Mariah ignored it with a steely glance. "I'm here to find out what you've done with my nephew, and this man"—she turned and gave the unfortunate clerk a biting glare—"says I'm not to be told."

The clerk tried unsuccessfully to fade into the carpet.

"What's the boy's name?"

"Joshua Brighton."

Mr. Stone's face lit up. "Oh, Joshua! What a splendid young man!"

Mariah sagged in relief. "Thank God. Now where can I find him?"

"That's a problem. He was on the orphan train—"

"Orphan train?" Mariah exploded.

"We take some children west to be adopted by farm families. It's good for them; nice clean air, honest work, and they're wanted out there."

"For slave labor!"

Mr. Stone swung his head slowly. "Oh no, miss. There you're wrong. These children are wanted and loved."

"Where is Joshua? I'll go out there and get him back."

"I'm sorry. I can't tell you that."

"Can't tell me that, or *won't* tell me that?" She glared contemptuously at the clerk cowering behind the counter. "I'll go get him and bring him back to civilization. I won't have him living in the middle of nowhere."

Mr. Stone leaned one elbow on the counter. "If an adoption has already taken place, we don't intervene unless there's some sort of difficulty within the family."

"There's difficulty within *this* family!"

"I mean the child and his adoptive family." He led her to the window. "Look out there."

Along the rain-splattered street, bits of paper littered the gutters and walkways. Mr. Stone pointed to a group of boys, no older than twelve, huddled with false braggadocio in a doorway, sharing a single cigarette.

"Chances are those boys are home right now."

"Home?"

"For many children, the street is the only home they know. We're trying to rectify that by sending as many of them as we can to good, solid farm families in the Midwest where they can grow up in a healthy environment."

Mariah watched one boy pull his collar up in a futile attempt to keep the rain off his neck. "I understand that, and I think it's commendable, but don't you see? Joshua doesn't need one of those homes. He already has one—with me."

"I'm sorry," he repeated. "We have our rules."

"Rules? I'll tell you what your rules are worth." She snapped her fingers. "This."

Angrily, Mariah spun on her heel and marched out of the room and onto the narrow walk that bordered the street. She paused outside the agency's door, oblivious to the droplets of rain that splattered her dress. Part of her wanted to burst into tears of defeat and disappointment, and the other part wanted to put her fist through the lettered window.

Fighting back the sobs that tightened her throat, she realized she still gripped the piece of paper in her hand that she had seized from the desk in Orphans and Foundlings.

It was torn, but enough remained to make her stop midstride. "Joshu—" The name sprang out at her. Below it were parts of letters that made no sense to her.

Except for a single word that stood alone at the bottom corner of the paper: *Fargo.*

Fargo? She'd heard the word before. Her breath caught as she remembered. Fargo was a place in the Dakota Territory, one of those towns that had sprung up during the Homestead Act years.

Her knees nearly buckled beneath her as she took in the implications. She had just discovered where to find Joshua, and it was the middle of nowhere.

Mariah had heard about the Dakota Territory. It was wild and untamed, precisely not the environment she wanted Joshua to grow up in. How could there be good homes out there in the absolute wilderness? Joshua was undoubtedly in danger.

Mariah didn't give it a second thought.

She turned in the direction of the train station. Wherever Joshua was out there in the Dakota Territory, she was going to go get him and bring him home from the nightmare called Fargo.

The *choo-ka-choo-ka-choo-ka* of the train wheels was hypnotic, but Mariah was too tense to fall under its spell. She pulled her bag closer to her feet and looked out the window as the fields sped by in a blur.

She was bound for the Dakota Territory. Her hand strayed to her skirt pocket and felt the reassuring outline of the crinkled paper with the cryptic clue. It wasn't much, but it was all she had.

It had been a long two days, the longest of her life.

Everything had started out so brightly. She'd appeared at her sister's boardinghouse, ready to surprise her. Her purse contained a bank book showing enough deposits to finally rescue Lorna and her son from the tenements of New York. It had taken almost three years of working eighteen-hour shifts in the mill at Lowell and doing stints at the sample shop next door, but she'd finally made it.

As long as she lived, though, she would never forget the numb feeling that overcame her as Lorna's landlady told her about Lorna's death from influenza shortly after Christmas and the agency that had taken Joshua away. In one short moment, everything in her life had been stripped from her, everyone she ever cared about, everything she had ever dreamed.

Mariah's mind drifted through scenes from Lorna's life. Lorna had taken being the older sister very seriously, and she told Mariah the best stories, acting out each of the parts.

She smiled as she recalled Lorna being George Washington, Martha Washington, and Lafayette reliving Valley Forge. When Mariah had mentioned that she didn't think Martha Washington had been at Valley

Forge, Lorna had waved away the objection, explaining that it was a lovely thing called "poetic license."

Most of the stories were Bible stories, however, and Lorna once told the story of Jesus and the money changers with such vigor that she'd knocked over an armoire. Her Nativity retelling, complete with an angelic lullaby for the newborn Jesus, would make Mariah weep every time.

When Mariah had been a rebellious adolescent, insisting that praying was silly because God already knew what she thought, Lorna had simply and sweetly said, as she knelt beside her bed for her evening prayers, "I pray your prayers, too."

Then their parents had died, and Lorna had taken care of Mariah, even delaying her own marriage to her childhood sweetheart until Mariah was safely on her own. When Lorna's husband passed away from an infection in his lungs, she and the child had been forced to live off what sparse earnings she could make selling notions in a department store.

The world without Lorna in it—it was almost too much to consider. And to think that Joshua, only five years old, was alone in the world. So small, so defenseless. After all that Lorna had done for her, Mariah knew that she had no choice—she had to do what her heart had ordered her to do. She had to find Joshua.

She leaned back against the hard leather of the train seat and shut her eyes. It was time to talk to God.

It was time to pray Lorna's prayers.

* * *

Ben stood outside the station. The plow part he needed was supposed to be on this train. If it wasn't, he'd have to delay even longer finishing up on the far section of cropland. That was only a small part of his acreage, but it bothered him to see it lay fallow for even this short period of time.

The train usually pulled in about this time each afternoon, but now that more people were coming to the territory, each car was pretty much filled by the time it arrived here in Fargo. And that meant more stops along the way, picking up those who were coming west to try their hand at homesteading.

He could wait. At least that's what he told himself as he forced himself to quit pacing the train yard and peering down the tracks. It wouldn't make any difference if he saw the train or not, and his anxiety wouldn't hurry the locomotive along. It would come whenever it came. That was the truth, and he might as well enjoy this time.

The sun was warm on his back, and he sank onto the unfinished wooden bench, slightly shaded by the portico where the loading and unloading from the train took place. He could have gone inside, that was true, into the depot, which was fine enough to make any town proud. No one could look at Fargo, Dakota Territory, and think it was a hick village. Not anymore.

Lars Olsen, a burly man who farmed near Ben, approached him, mopping at his forehead with a hand-ker-chief. His face was red with a persistent sunburn under his white-blond hair.

"Warm today," he commented and with a sigh, lowered himself onto the bench beside Ben.

"It is that," Ben agreed. "But I'm not complaining. You know that soon enough we'll be remembering these summer days while we grouse about the winter weather."

"Yup, yup, yup, yup." Lars grinned. "But you take away our ability to whine and moan about the weather, and we Dakotans aren't going to have anything to talk about." Lars had a faint Norwegian accent that came out when he wasn't careful, and Ben found it amusing to hear "ve Dakotans."

Ben chuckled in response. "That's true. After church, we'd all be standing around, looking at each other and wondering what we might think of to say to each other. Down at Meggin's shop, there'd be nobody gathered in the corner by the pickle barrel because we'd have nothing to discuss."

They both laughed. Meggin Sanders owned the store in Prospect, the little town near both men's homesteads, and the mercantile was a daily congregation point for the men, who found the large pickle barrel a convenient spot to rally each day. Some men were brave enough to put their feet on the top of the barrel, teasingly inviting Meggin to come over and whap their dusty boots with her ever-present towel.

"So what are you doing in Fargo?" Lars asked. "If I'd known you were coming, I'd have hitched a ride with you. It's a long ride from Prospect. You got someone coming in on the train?"

"No, not a some*one* but a some*thing*. The bolt that

holds the plow assemblage on just simply sheared off. Had to order a new one."

Lars swabbed his forehead again. "Aw, that'll stop a man dead in his tracks. Did you have to wait long for it?"

"Two weeks. Could have been longer, but Reverend Timms's brother was visiting, and he was on his way back to St. Paul, and he got the part for me and had it shipped on."

"That's a piece of luck, indeed. Still, it's too bad you had to come all this way for that one bit. I could have got it for you. One day, they'll be able to put something like that in a box and send it so it'll come to you, not you having to spend almost a full day coming to pick it up and then going back home."

"That day isn't going to happen in my lifetime or yours," Ben said with a laugh. "Not unless they can create a wagon that moves as fast as the wind, or make a train that doesn't need tracks."

"I suppose."

"So," Ben asked him, "are you waiting for the train, too?"

Lars nodded. "I told Meggin I'd pick up a box for her." His ruddy face grew even pinker. "Some gewgaws for the ladies, I guess, hot off the presses of *Godey's Lady's Book*. She wouldn't tell me what it was about, and I promised not to look inside. Plus Lionel Elderson asked me to pick up his saddle while I was here—he's having it mended down the street there—and the Ladies' Aid wanted to know if I would check on the price of a new set of silverware for them since apparently they're down to sixteen spoons."

Ben laughed. "Sounds like you should start your own transit business!"

"Well, it's a beautiful day. The Lord doesn't make them all this good, so I'm glad to spend it here. You're coming back tonight?"

"No," Ben answered. "I'm going to stay over. They've got one of those traveling preachers coming through, and I thought I'd sit in and listen. I can get home tomorrow just fine."

"One can never hear too much of the Word, that's for sure," Lars declared. "Oh, look at that. Here's the train, and only a bit late."

With a great squealing of brakes and dark puffs of smoke, the train pulled to a stop. Lars said something to Ben that was lost in the cacophony of the locomotive and ambled off.

The doors of the passenger car opened, and the occupants poured out. Most of them, Ben knew, would use this as a chance to stretch their legs before returning to the train and continuing on their trip, but it was still amazing to him to see how many people were still coming west. How many would stay? It was impossible to know.

A woman stepped off the train and stumbled slightly as her foot touched the platform. Instinctively Ben stepped forward, but she recovered her balance and tilted her chin upward a fraction of an inch.

She was dressed in a dove-gray traveling suit, the tailored lines creased by wrinkles apparently caused by long hours of riding in the train. Her red hair caught the late-afternoon sun and glittered like bright copper under the small black velvet hat perched atop her head.

His brow wrinkled as he watched her gather her bags around her and then stand beside them, her eyes indecisively scanning the knots of people assembled on the platform.

Whoever she was, she was beautiful and elegant… and judging from the circles under her eyes, incredibly spent.

Mariah's head spun as she surveyed the crowd of people that swirled around her. She couldn't imagine being more tired. The train's fumes added to her lightheadedness.

So this was Dakota.

Two men emerged from the station, rough, unshaven characters wearing undershirts and stained work trousers held up by suspenders. They laughed raucously as they headed her way.

She tried to sidestep them, but a cluster of people prevented her from moving. One of the two men bumped into her, nearly knocking her from her feet. He righted himself and grinned at her. His breath stank of liquor.

"Sorry, ma'am," he said, swaying to the side. "I'm a bit unsteady on my feet today."

Mariah cringed as he patted her arm.

"Anyhoo," he continued, smiling happily, "welcome to Fargo, home of the best—" He waved his arm in a loose circle. "Well, I don't know what it's the home of, but I'm sure it's the best. I'm from here, and I'm the best drunk in the territory!"

A man sitting on a nearby bench rose to his feet, probably to chase the men away from her, but before he could intervene, the two inebriated men tipped their hats to her, linked arms, and walked away.

He crossed the wooden planking to where she stood. "May I be of assistance?"

She turned to face him.

"Could you direct me to a rooming house?" Mariah asked as she studied the man who stood beside her. He was nearly six feet tall, and under hair the color of ripe wheat, his eyes were the same clear blue as the Dakota sky.

"Rooming house?"

"Or a hotel." A lock of copper-red hair strayed across her forehead, and she mindlessly tucked it back under the velvet scrap that served as her hat.

"You're traveling alone?" he asked her, and she pushed away the image of the two men who had accosted her.

"If it's my safety you're concerned about," she said, drawing herself up to her full five feet, two and a quarter inches of height, "I can take care of myself."

"I don't doubt that." He smiled, revealing even, white teeth. "Actually, Fargo has several fine hotels, but if you plan to stay awhile…" His words trailed off into an unspoken question.

She looked around her disdainfully. "I hope not."

He shrugged. "Then perhaps the folks you're visiting can help you," he said, and he started to walk away.

"I'm not visiting anyone."

He stopped. "Well, if you've come to homestead, all the claims are taken. In these parts, anyway," he hastily amended.

"I won't be homesteading."

She was completely done in. Right now her brain was clouded from exhaustion. More than anything, she craved a room where she could remove her shoes and lie on a bed and let sleep claim her weary mind. And she wanted it soon.

Mariah shifted the small bag she held impatiently. "If you could just direct me to the nearest hotel, I'd be grateful."

The man rubbed his hand over his thick mustache and paused.

But he paused a bit too long. Mariah's temper, worn thin with exhaustion, burst. "Look, I'm tired. I've been traveling for a long time, and I need some sleep." As if to prove her point, her knees weakened, and she swayed slightly but righted herself before the man's quickly outstretched hand could steady her.

"How long are you staying?"

"I'm not sure." Why was he taking so long? And why was he asking her so many questions?

"The thing is that right now there's a shortage of rooms here, and while you might be able to get one for a night or two, anything longer term than that could be a problem."

That was a problem. A huge problem.

Mariah took a deep breath. Even though she was tired, she might as well begin her search now. This man seemed friendly enough. Perhaps he knew something about Joshua—but she needed to proceed carefully. The man at Orphans and Foundlings had been resistant to giving her any information, and if his demeanor was any indication of what she would be up against in looking for Joshua, she'd have to be ready to tackle some folks who didn't want to help her.

The fact was that she should be prepared to be here for an extended period of time.

She chose her words carefully. "Is there an option for someone who might be here longer? Someone such as I?"

The man smiled and stuck his hand out. "I think there might be. We should be introduced. I'm Ben Harris. I farm out by Prospect, which is southeast of here, down past Wahpeton."

She nodded. She had seen the map.

"I'm Mariah Rose, and I'm glad to meet you."

"Here's the situation," Ben explained. "My neighbor and his wife have been called back to Wisconsin for a year, and he needs someone to look after his place."

"His place?" she asked warily.

"His farm."

"I don't know anything about taking care of a farm," Mariah said.

Ben laughed. "You don't have to. I'm taking care of the livestock and the fields. He just needs someone to stay in the house."

"Why?"

"A house unoccupied for very long out here soon goes back to the land. He's put a lot into the house, and he doesn't want to lose it. It'll be vacant for at least a year, so if you're planning to stay the winter, you'd be mighty welcome to stay there."

Stay the winter. She resisted a shudder.

Mariah chewed her lip.

"I can offer you another incentive," Ben added. "It's free—no rent."

Mariah mentally took inventory of her purse's contents. The one thing she didn't have was much money. The train trip had consumed most of her meager savings.

Ben must have noticed her hesitation. He said, "I know you're tired. I'll show you to a hotel, and you can get some sleep there tonight. Then tomorrow, I'll drive you out to the farm. You can look at it yourself and make the decision. If it's not right for you, I'll bring you back into town in the evening."

"How far away is it?"

"Little over five hours."

Mariah knew that if she weren't so exhausted, she wouldn't find the plan acceptable. But right now, her thoughts could go no further than a clean bed and a hot bath.

"All right."

Ben scooped up her bags and walked with her down the street. The sight of Fargo surprised Mariah. It wasn't as small as she'd imagined. Brick buildings as large as many she'd seen in Lowell lined the main street, and the people walking in front of them were a curious mixture—some were dressed in ranch clothing while others were quite fashionably clad.

In the setbacks from the street were the most beautiful lilacs she had ever seen. Big and glorious and fragrant, they added a level of grace to this dusty prairie town. She had never seen any lilacs like this before. They were immense, and the whole street smelled of their perfume.

He led her inside one of the largest buildings and stopped. "This is the best hotel. I'd better not go to the desk with you, or tongues will be wagging for sure."

Mariah reddened at his words, but he seemed not to notice. Instead, he touched the brim of his hat, nodded slightly, and said, "I'll pick you up here in the lobby at eight tomorrow morning, if that's fine with you."

She nodded.

He left, but she was too busy looking around the interior of the hotel to take much note of his departure. The lobby was spacious and clean, much more than she had expected in such a cow town.

The young man at the desk glanced at her with only slight curiosity as he held the register out for her to sign.

She stiffened at the price of the room. This night would be her one luxury in her search for Joshua; she could not afford any more.

For what she was paying to stay at the hotel, she might as well get some information, she decided. "Do you know anything about the orphan train that came through here a while back? A couple of months or so ago?" she asked the clerk. "It might even have been longer. I don't know for sure."

He scratched behind his ear. "Well, sure. Went and

saw it myself. Too bad those poor little tykes didn't have homes back East, but at least now they've got good ones here."

Mariah chose her words carefully. With the disapproval of Orphans and Foundlings behind her, she might have a hard time getting Joshua back, or even finding out where he was.

"Were any of them placed here in Fargo?" She dared not breathe as she awaited his answer.

He shook his head. "Nope. They went to farm homes, every single one of them. I heard folks came from all over this part of the territory to take a gander at the little ones. But there's supposed to be another bunch coming in next spring. Maybe you could get one of them."

Mariah cringed inside at his choice of words. He made it sound as if children were a mere commodity on the market. Nor could she explain that she didn't want *one of them*. There was only one child she wanted, and he was Joshua.

"No," she said, suddenly weak. "No."

He shrugged his shoulders and signaled to a young man to carry her bags.

The room she was shown to was well-appointed. Carpet patterned in muted greens reflected the deep-forest coloring of the spread on the heavy brass bed, which looked deliciously inviting after nearly three days in a train seat.

A large painting dominated the far wall. It was a sunlit pastoral scene in which a tunic-clad shepherd piped happily while sheep as cottony white as clouds grazed on even, green grass. It was aptly suitable art-work for the room, but the vista didn't seem to have anything to do with the Dakota Territory, which looked brand-new and raw instead of cleanly classical.

She turned her attention to the rest of the room. Thick curtains draped the windows, cutting out the edges of sunlight, and the washbasin and pitcher atop the bureau were dust-free and unchipped.

Everything was spotlessly neat. Of course, she re-minded herself, it was new—just as everything here would be new. In a few months, she was sure, it would be range-bitten like the men she'd seen at the station.

She pulled the piece of paper from her pocket and laid it on top of her Bible.

She'd placed all her faith in this scrap, but the fact was there was no assurance that the Joshua on the paper was her nephew, or that he had come here. There could have been other boys named Joshua, and *Fargo* didn't necessarily mean he'd been adopted here.

But she needed something to believe in, something to move her forward out of the grief that still threat-ened to overwhelm her.

She needed it to be true.

With her fingers resting on the tiny bit of paper, she did the only thing she could do. She turned to her Lord and prayed out loud. "Please, dearest God, dear-est, dearest God, lead me to him. He must be terrified. I know I am. He's lost his mother and—"

She couldn't go further. She put her head down, on top of the paper, but she couldn't cry. She didn't even know it was possible to hurt so bad that the tears would not come, but there she was.

Somewhere this very moment, Joshua was sleeping, not in Fargo, if the fellow at the desk downstairs was to be believed, but somewhere near. It was almost too much for her to bear. She wanted to spring up and search for him, to knock on every single door in the territory until she found him.

But what she needed now was sleep. Mariah dropped onto the bed, and within minutes she was fast asleep.

In a room two stories up in the same hotel, Ben was wide awake. He paced the length of his sleeping quarters, trying to get the image of Mariah Rose out of his head.

Why had she come to Dakota? She didn't look at all comfortable with the environment. Certainly there were differences between the East Coast and the territory, but most people who came out here knew to expect them.

Maybe that was it. Maybe what bothered him was that he sensed she had arrived prepared to hate the Dakota Territory. But that led him back to his original question: Why, then, had she come out here?

He didn't intend to ask, either. People came for a variety of reasons, almost all of them beginning with the notion of starting over again. Folks here didn't ask too many questions. Secrets of a man's—or a woman's—past were revealed when that person wanted to disclose them, not before.

But somehow Ben knew that her reasons for being in the Dakota Territory were tied in with whatever had washed the color from her cheeks, and whatever had made those tiny lines around her eyes.

For some reason, he cared. Already, he cared.

Was he foolish? He'd asked a woman he didn't know to move into his neighbors' house. As soon as the words had flown out of his mouth, though, his heart felt good about it. It was right.

He'd never be able to explain it, but it was right.

He wandered over to the window and gazed out. From his position he could see the night prairie, wonderful in its starlit glory, every inch of it singing the Creator's praises. Would she ever see that in the land?

It was important that she did, very important indeed.

A pounding at the door intruded into Mariah's dreams. She stumbled to her feet and opened the door a crack.

Ben Harris stood outside.

"Oh, I'm sorry, ma'am," he said, looking at a spot on the doorframe. "I thought we said eight o'clock."

"What time is it?" she mumbled, her mind starting to function.

"Eight-thirty." His voice was apologetic.

Suddenly Mariah was wide awake.

"Give me a few minutes. I'll meet you in the lobby."

She'd woken up at daybreak, gotten dressed, fixed her hair, and laid back down for just a moment, and apparently had fallen back asleep.

Mariah repacked her bags, all the while preparing a thousand reasons not to go with him, but every one of them paled when she thought of her dwindling resources. Besides, what could it hurt to look at this land? And maybe he could tell her something about the orphan train.

So she met him downstairs and allowed herself to follow him outside into the bright morning sunlight.

Ben led her to a wagon. He helped her onto the buckboard, and then he leaped up beside her and took the reins, and with a quick "Tch" to the horses, they were off.

They left Fargo and were soon on the open prairie. They had been riding along in silence as she studied the austere landscape, when suddenly she was jolted out of her seat.

"It's a little bumpy," he apologized.

Mariah scanned the area outside Fargo. As far as her eyes could see, there was only flat prairie. Apparently they had hit the only bump in Dakota, she told herself wryly. Maybe it was some kind of landmark.

"One of my favorite things about Dakota is the sky," Ben remarked conversationally. "I don't know where else you could find that color. And the clouds are the fluffiest, whitest things you'll ever see."

Mariah looked up. Only one thin cloud stretched across a corner of the sky. "First of all, I don't see any clouds. Second of all, this sky is entirely too big."

He laughed. "Ma'am, the sky is much bigger than even what you see here. Why, it stretches all the way to China."

"I know that," she answered testily. "But you know what I mean."

"By the way, the farm we're going to is near a town called Prospect. It's just starting up, but it has a lot of potential. I think you'll like it."

Mariah looked at him darkly. The chances that she'd like anything in this wasteland were slim at best, but if she spoke too freely of her opinion of the Dakota Territory, she might not be able to stay at this house.

And she had to. For Joshua.

The ride seemed endless, as infinite as the land that spread from horizon to horizon and the sky that arched overhead. She felt suddenly small and vulnerable, a lonely spot in this great openness. She shivered, glancing around her nervously.

"What are you looking for?" Ben asked.

"Indians." It wasn't exactly true, but it was easier than trying to explain the odd sensation that had overtaken her.

He threw back his head and hooted with laughter. Affronted, Mariah straightened up on the buckboard. "What is so amusing? There are Indians here, right?"

Ben nodded. "Of course. But the Lakota are no problem."

"*No problem?* But what about the scalping, the massacres, the—"

He held up his hand to stop her. "No scalping, no massacres. The Lakota are good, fine people." He grew serious and stared ahead thoughtfully. "Though I don't see why they haven't been angrier. I know I'd be if someone took my land."

"It's not the same thing," Mariah objected. "And they should be grateful, not upset. After all, we're bringing them civilization."

Ben brought the wagon to a halt. "There's civilization, and then there's civilization, Mariah. And from what I know of the Lakota, I sometimes think they know more about the meaning of the word than we do."

"But they're savages!"

"Absolutely not. Savage can be the way one acts or thinks. But to say the Lakota are savage because they look different or have different ways is totally wrong." He picked up the reins and urged the horses on again. "Not that it'll matter in a practical sense anyway. The chances you'll run into a Lakota on the farm are slim. But I would recommend you rethink your feelings."

Mariah thought about what he had said as they rode quietly on. There was a ring of truth to it. She didn't know anything about the native people who lived here. All she'd heard was rumor.

Nevertheless, she'd take comfort in his prediction that she wouldn't encounter any of the people he called the Lakota. Besides, there were undoubtedly more menaces on this flat new land, some not as obvious as the others. Menaces she had to rescue Joshua from.

The prairie darkened momentarily, and Mariah looked up. The cloud that had been a faint thread across the sky only moments earlier had drifted across the sun.

Mariah shuddered involuntarily at the omen, but

almost immediately the sun shot through the cloud and washed the prairie with early summer sunshine.

She was in Dakota.

Chapter 2

Ben and Mariah rode by a few small towns on their way to Prospect—at least Mariah assumed they were what passed as small towns out here. They were little more than groups of raw new buildings huddled together as if seeking protection from the perils of the wild prairie.

All around them the wind blew. Nothing stopped its path, and it never let up. She wrapped her scarf tighter and pulled it forward to shield her eyes from its onslaught.

As they jounced along on the wagon, the regularity of the horses' hoofbeats on the dirt road lulled her mind, and her thoughts returned to Joshua.

Somewhere out here was her nephew.

When she had last seen him, he had just memorized

his alphabet. Would his new family know how much he loved to learn? Would they recognize that he had the potential to become a doctor or a lawyer?

She surveyed the open land in scorn. How could people in this wasteland stress education when all their efforts had to be channeled into scraping a living off the soil? There weren't even any trees out here, except for a few scraggly cottonwoods that dotted the landscape here and there.

"Prospect's right ahead," Ben said, interrupting her reverie.

Mariah sat forward on the hard wooden seat and strained her eyes to see what he was pointing at. She could barely make out a bump on the horizon.

"That's Prospect?" she asked, frowning.

Ben nodded proudly. "Best little town in the Dakota Territory."

"How 'little' is it?" Trepidation filled her voice.

"Oh, maybe one hundred and fifty, if you count the households from the surrounding area that use Prospect."

"How do they use Prospect? Does it have a school?"

He looked at her curiously. "Are you a teacher?"

She shook her head. "Seamstress."

"The school used to meet at the church, but Lainie, the woman who lived in the house where you're staying, was the teacher. Since she left, the young ones have been going to Mackenzie Township, which is quite a distance from here. I told Olea she should do it," he informed her with a sly grin. "She knows everything, or thinks she does. You know how big sisters are."

She did, and the memory of Lorna guiding her through life struck her heart like a knife.

She turned the conversation back to him. "Olea's your sister?"

"Yup. She's older than me, which means that in her eyes I'm still a stripling barely out of short pants. You have any sisters or brothers?"

Mariah thought about Lorna, and about her mission here in the territory. "I had an older sister," she said faintly, trying to block the memory of Lorna's gentle smile and her warm, laughing eyes.

He glanced at her, an unspoken question in his eyes, but she dropped her gaze, pretending to settle her skirt over her knees.

He looked back toward the horses and urged them onward.

Soon he turned the wagon down a side road. "We'll stop at my house first, if you don't mind. I don't know about you, but I could use a cool drink."

Mariah nodded. The water they'd shared from the glass jar balanced between them had gone brackish with the day's heat, and she drank it only out of necessity.

He pulled up in front of a large house that gleamed white in the afternoon sun. It looked recently painted, and Mariah realized that the entire house was new. It was actually quite grand, even by East Coast standards.

On the large porch that surrounded the first floor,

several chairs were placed. The windows were open, and red-and-white-checked curtains caught the slight breeze that drifted across the yard.

He helped her down from the wagon and led her to the front door.

It opened into the parlor. It was a typical man's room, with brightly colored throws covering sturdy heavy pine furniture. The only things she hadn't expected were the shelves of books that lined two walls.

Ben excused himself to get them some tea, and in his absence, Mariah examined the titles on the volumes. They surprised her: plays by Shakespeare, philosophical works by Plato and Aristotle, a Bible, and a thick volume of English poetry. She hadn't figured Ben to be the literary type.

Ben returned with two glasses of tea.

"Ice!" Mariah exclaimed.

"I have an ice house. I cut ice in the winter, and it usually lasts all summer long."

Mariah drank deeply. It seemed as if all the road dust had gone into her throat, and the iced tea certainly helped wash it away.

He glanced at the clock that ticked loudly on the mantel. "We should probably go to the other house," he said.

Out on the porch, he motioned across the field. "There's the farmstead there," he told her. "Finish your tea, and we'll go over there. The horses should be somewhat rested by now."

"Why take the horses?" she asked. "Let's walk. It

can't be that far." Her back ached from the long wagon ride, and she longed to stretch out by walking.

"Out here, distances can be deceiving. It's at least a mile away, more probably two."

Mariah squinted against the sun. "It doesn't look that far."

He laughed. "Trust me. I've trekked back and forth between these two houses every day for the last three months. It's a long way away."

This was just another strange thing about the Dakota Territory, Mariah thought as they rode to what might become her new home. Nothing was ever quite what she expected.

And she certainly never expected to see what met her eyes when Ben pulled into the yard.

Weather-beaten boards made up the exterior of the small house, and the ground was splotchy with grass and dirt. Everywhere she looked, she saw neglect and defeat.

She climbed down from the wagon and wandered around the bare front yard.

"Karl had to let some things slide when his wife got sick," Ben said, noting her dismay.

"She was sick?" Mariah asked, idly fingering the limp leaf of a nearly dead apple tree seedling.

"In the family way," he answered briefly. "That's why they went to Wisconsin."

Mariah's eyes shot to his. "She had to go Wisconsin to have a baby? Aren't there any doctors here?" This was something else to blacken Dakota's image in her mind.

Ben looked uneasy. "Well, sure we have doctors. Lainie just wanted to be with her kinfolk when her time came."

Mariah understood the woman's reasoning. The same thought had driven her out here to find Joshua and bring him safely back home.

Ben opened the door. "Why don't you look around inside while I see to the livestock?"

The small house was actually one large room, divided by a single blanket strung across ropes. She explored curiously.

The room in its entirety was no more than twelve feet square. The walls were made of planed pine. Someone had tried to whitewash the boards, and the untreated plank had absorbed the paint unevenly, leaving the walls stippled white and brown.

She ran her fingers across the furred surface of the boards. The grooves left by the planing blades were faint—a sign of good millwork.

She turned her attention to the rest of the room. A black cast-iron stove hunkered in one corner, and beside it shelves were filled with clear bottles of preserved vegetables and berries. Their cheerful ruby, topaz, and emerald colors provided the only spots of brightness in that part of the room.

Under the shelves a little table was pushed against the wall, with two straight-back chairs neatly centered on each end. Blue and white dishes were stacked in a precise pile in the middle of the table.

She put her hand on the table, and when she lifted it, the imprint remained. A fine layer of dust covered everything, a result of the wind that had been blowing relentlessly all day and had only now quieted to a gentle breeze.

She was pleased to notice that the windows were glass, not the waxy paper she had heard was being used instead of the expensive panes that had to be imported by train or wagon from the East.

The only other concession to the amenities she had known back East was the bed. Despite the dust, the brass headboard shone, and the wedding-ring quilt that graced the top of it combined muted pastels into a harmonious palette. The seamstress in her came out, and she examined the quilt closely. Each tiny stitch was even and strong, and when she turned it over, the pattern emerged through the stitchery. This, she knew, was the mark of a good seamstress.

A blanket was strung across one corner of the room. She lifted the flap curiously and discovered a large washtub and a discreet bowl and pitcher. She'd seen an outhouse when they drove up, so the chinaware must be for those times when going outside was impossible. Involuntarily she shuddered at what those times would have been. The Dakota Territory's winters were notorious on the East Coast. According to her landlady in Lowell, the cold was so severe that thermometers would burst. She'd have to ask Ben about that. Not that it would matter, of course; she wouldn't be here long enough to see a change of seasons.

Her eyes were drawn to the opposite corner. There, tucked into the junction of two walls, was a bracketed shelf. The board had been cut into a triangle so the shelf nestled securely without either end extending into the room. It was an incredibly economical use of the limited space the house offered.

The shelf displayed a small ceramic cube. The top was hinged, and inside were the workings of a music box. She wound it, and the strains of Strauss's "Blue Danube Waltz" filled the room.

Mariah felt a kinship with the woman who had lived there, "Lainie" Ben had called her. She, too, must have been drawn away from the civilized surroundings of the East Coast, perhaps New York or Boston. Was this her memento, the only thing she could bring with her as a reminder of her old life?

No wonder it occupied such a spot of honor.

But why had she left it? Had she been in such a hurry to leave that she had forgotten it? Or had it lost its meaning?

Mariah sank onto the bed, still holding the music box. Questions tumbled through her head like tumbleweeds caught in the wild Dakota wind. Why had the woman left the security of her home to come to such an untamed place? Could it have been out of love for her husband? Mariah could not imagine such a thing. No love could conquer this wilderness.

When Ben walked into the house, Mariah was still sitting on the bed, the music box in her hand.

"Made up your mind yet?" he asked.

She looked around her with a kind of despair. This was not where she wanted to bring Joshua, but at the same time she had to remember that even if she found him, she couldn't take him back home right away. She didn't have enough money for train fare for both of them to return to Massachusetts immediately.

"Is there any way I can make some money out here?" she asked bluntly.

"Meggin Sanders was just mentioning the other day that she can't sew fast enough to keep up with the demand. She runs the store in Prospect. I'd think you could probably do that, if you wanted to."

Mariah took one more look around. If for no other reason than to honor the woman who had left this, her home, to have a baby, she would stay. She would improve it as best she could, too. This woman named Lainie would return to a house that was put to rights for a woman who was now a mother. It didn't matter if she was on the prairie or in the midst of the finest hotel in New York City—she deserved more.

She would do it in honor of her sister, who had to have died with fear in her veins about what would become of her beloved son.

"All right," she said to Ben. "I'll stay." Then she faced him. "But I must tell you one thing. I've come out here with a purpose, and as soon as I've accomplished it, I'll be leaving."

An expression that she couldn't read rushed across his face, there and gone so quickly that she had no idea what it was, no idea what he felt. Time seemed to hold its breath, measured only by the faint sawing of grasshoppers and the trilling of a meadowlark, and she waited for him to fill the void with an explanation.

His eyes, bluer even than the afternoon sky—Scandinavian blue, she thought—were locked onto her own, and she didn't move, waiting for him to speak.

At last he turned, saying merely, "I'll unload the wagon."

She clasped her fingers together tightly around the music box. This was not the answer she'd wanted to hear.

Ben dropped the reins lightly on Old Gray's back. The horse was so used to the routine that he started right up, headed for the barn he knew as home.

Sunlight washed across Ben's face, and he lifted his hat and dropped it onto the seat beside him, just to welcome the warmth. Thinking was easier, he thought, when the sun shone square on a fellow's face.

And he had a lot of thinking to do.

So she had made those elegant clothes she wore, he mused. Then she probably wasn't rich after all. That was a piece of the puzzle—a small piece. She had worked as a seamstress.

He had wanted to ask her why she'd inquired about a school if she wasn't a teacher, but he'd held back. Whatever she wanted to tell him, she would, in due time.

Ben noticed the way Mariah's face had closed when she'd spoken of her sister, but not before he caught a glimpse of raw, still-new grief written in her eyes. A wash of sympathy broke over him just remembering, but he wouldn't speak of it. He knew she needed her silence yet.

There was something in the defiant way she spoke

that brushed Ben's heart, and for the first time he realized that what she was facing was not easy for her, not easy at all.

What it was, he had no idea. Something had brought her out here, something major enough to convince her to leave her home and come to what she perceived as a wild land ready to pounce on her.

There were three kinds of people, he reckoned, that came to Dakota. Four, if he included himself.

First, there were the adventurers, those called by the lure of the open land. He'd met many a fellow out here who had come west solely for the chance to be his own man on his own property. The chance to carve out a piece of the earth and call it home—it was like a magnet to many folks.

He dismissed this as the reason she'd come out here.

Others came because they were fleeing a criminal past. He had met some of those people, too—men who'd traveled west to escape a sure and certain life behind the bars of a prison. In many cases, they'd left their behavior in the East and started again with new resolve. And, of course, there were those who saw the chance to make some money off the unsuspecting newcomers. Society would always have folks like that, those who thought only of how to bilk others out of their belongings, money, or property.

He figured that wasn't the reason she'd come out here. He almost laughed at the idea of Mariah as a criminal.

The third group came out of desperation, because they had nothing else to do, no place to go. Poverty had forced them out of the big cities from homes they could no longer afford. Here, maybe, a man had a chance to make a go of it. Maybe he could provide a home for his family; maybe he could throw off the burden of need and hold his head up.

Mariah didn't look poor, not at all, although she'd intimated that money was a concern.

She was a woman of contradictions, though; he was no judge of women's wear, but what she wore looked to him to be expensive, with jeweled buttons and ruffles and ribbons and some fancy gold twirly things on the collar that he didn't know the name of.

That left the fourth group, the one he was in. It was made of people who simply swept along with others, who came with family members or friends. That was how he'd gotten here.

Olea, always the big sister watching after her little brother, had swept him up in the plan she and her husband Fred had concocted. It would be good, she'd told him, for so many reasons. The land. The *free* land. The good farming—and before he could counter with the fact that he'd never farmed in his life, she'd pointed out that all one had to do was simply fling seeds on the ground, and the next thing you knew, you were bringing in the sheaves promised in the psalm.

She hadn't been quite right about that, but she was right about the last point she'd made: he had needed Dakota.

Oh, he hadn't been in trouble, or overly idle—although he did like sprawling on the rocking chair on the porch as much as the next guy—but he had been directionless, going nowhere, simply waiting for something to come along and fill him with energy.

That *something* had been the Dakota Territory.

He'd been rootless. Now, he felt his own roots reaching into the land as strongly as the thready wheat roots that began small and over the growing season reached deeply into the soil, roots that went deeper into the rich earth of Dakota than he could even imagine.

Something about this part of the world spoke to the empty place in him. *Fill this spot with something beautiful,* it said to him. He'd gathered images of astonishing splendor: a sunrise over a still-sleeping field, the wings of a yellow butterfly on a pink prairie rose, the melodic trill of a meadowlark on a summer afternoon.

Even that, though, hadn't been enough, until one Sunday night, after spending the day in church with Olea and Fred, he'd been unable to sleep and wandered outside. Moonlight washed across the land, bathing the entire scene that surrounded him—earth and sky both—with a deep and clear blue, not indigo exactly, not cerulean, but a blue that was so liquid, it seemed to be poured over it all.

He had always considered himself a religious man, a truly God-fearing man, who did what the Bible and his teachers told him to do. God Himself had been a distant ruler, and His Son, Jesus, wasn't much closer—but they were both to be respected and obeyed.

However, in that blue-drenched moment, when the

prairie was soaked with beauty, he took one step closer to knowing who had created it, and was creating it still.

He wasn't perfect—oh, far from it—but every day he tried to shorten the distance between himself and his God. One day, the knowledge would be perfect.

His mind drifted back to his new neighbor.

Would Mariah ever see it? Did she long for God the way he did? Would she see Him in the prairie? Her eyes were alive with a native intelligence, so the possibility was definitely there.

Soon Old Gray had led him back to the homestead. Ben unhooked him and led him to the barn to be wiped down and fed.

Ben rubbed the horse's nose. "I think she'll be all right," he whispered into the animal's ear. "She's new at this, but she looks to be a quick learner."

The horse whinnied softly, and Ben chuckled. "I suppose you're right, Old Gray. We'll give her some room to learn our ways, and soon enough she'll love this place like we do."

For some reason, it mattered very much to him that she see the beauty in Dakota, but something had closed her soul to the wonders of the prairie. Whatever it was, it was important to her, and Ben knew that the best thing he could do was to let her work it out herself.

The horse nudged Ben's pocket, and he laughed. "Yes, I have your treat." He dipped into his pocket and then held his hand open while the horse snuffled against his palm until the sugar was gone.

Walking back to his house, Ben realized that, for some crazy reason, he was smiling.

* * *

After Ben had gone, Mariah unpacked her clothes and hung them in the small closet by the bed. There was so much to do that she was nearly overwhelmed.

What she needed was a nice, civilized cup of tea.

Ben had primed the pump beside the front door, but it still took several tries before she drew water.

She laid some wood in the stove and lit it with a match from the box on the shelf. The teakettle was dusty, so Mariah used some of the water to rinse it off.

Getting a cup of tea had never been so much trouble, but soon, a cup of steaming tea in her hand, she sat in the center of her new home.

Through the window she could see the sun setting in a blaze of glorious colors. It was almost as if, having been given as much room as possible, the sun was pouring its most dazzling shades of gold and purple onto the horizon.

As night fell, the air became cooler, but Mariah made no move. Her mind was busy as thoughts of Joshua tumbled around with questions about Ben.

He seemed so gentle and sensitive that he should have been out of place in this untamed country. Yet he fit in well, as if he and the land were two halves of a whole, partners in this curious venture called farming.

And what kind of man would willingly take on the extra duties involved with seeing to another man's farm while trying to scrape a living off his own plot of dirt?

Questions, questions, as endless as the prairie sunset.

When at last the house was cloaked in darkness, Mariah laid down on the bed, a light coverlet over her.

But although she shut her eyes, the events of the past few days kept spinning in her head like a Dakota dust storm.

Finally, unable to sleep, she left the room and stood outside the door. The sky had never seemed bigger, the stars brighter. She felt like a small speck on the face of the earth, perhaps the only speck, alone and defenseless on this endless prairie. Everything was bigger than she was. The prairie, the sky, even God Himself.

The urge to bolt nearly overpowered her. But the thought of Joshua, alone and abandoned, stayed her. Whatever it took, she would remain in this spot of nowhere until she found him.

"Joshua," she said aloud to the brightest star centered over the cottonwood, "if I have to look in every window or knock on every door in this land, I swear to you, I will find you. Lorna, this is my promise to you."

And, for the first time since the discovery of her sister's death, Mariah wept.

She woke the next morning strangely refreshed. As she prepared a breakfast of tea and bread, she noticed that the silence of the country was not silence at all, but a total cacophony of bird songs, insect hums, and leaves rustling in the wind.

She wandered outside and stretched. She had given the grounds only a cursory examination the day before, so she went to look at the garden.

It was behind the house, a large garden flourishing amid a tangle of weeds.

Mariah bent over one row and examined a section of

pale-green shoots for several minutes before straightening up. It was no use—she couldn't tell a radish sprout from ragweed. All her vegetables in Lowell had come from the greengrocer down the street.

But it was clear that the garden had to be weeded.

She walked around the garden until she stood at the south end. If she closed one eye, she could make out a faint pattern of greens. As she studied the design, lines of lighter green stood out against the random placement of the darker shades.

And thus she evolved her method of attack.

She would remove anything that was not in the pale-green lines, and if she pulled up cucumbers to allow dandelions free range, well, so be it.

Mariah rolled up her sleeves and dropped to her knees. As she tugged at dandelions and unwrapped bindweed from neighboring plants, she hummed under her breath and muttered softly at the weeds that seemed determined to remain despite her efforts.

She grabbed one particularly large plant and suddenly released it. Her hand flew to her mouth, and she stamped her foot as she sucked on her finger and tried to make the stinging stop.

"A good rule of thumb is never to grab Russian thistle with your bare hands," Ben said from behind her.

Mariah took her hand out of her mouth and looked at it. "Good heavens, what is *on* that plant?"

Ben leaned over and pushed the large weed on its side with his boot. "See these tiny little prickles along the stem? That's what got you."

"So what do I do now?" she asked.

"You try to get as many of the nasty little things out of your hand as you can." He lifted her hand and held it to the sunlight. "The tricky thing is seeing them. They're almost transparent."

He ran his finger along the inside of her hand. "I can feel a few. I know where Karl and Lainie kept their medical supplies. You sit here, and I'll go get it."

"Medical supplies?" she repeated to his back as he walked into the house. She glanced at her stinging hand and grumbled, "Somehow I am not surprised that my first morning here I need medical assistance."

He returned with a small metal box. From it he withdrew a pair of tweezers, and, taking her hand again, he bent his head over her fingers and began to pull the prickles out.

He knelt only inches from her, and he smelled like soap and bay rum man's cologne. A smile curved her lips as she wondered if he had put it on especially for her. It was flattering, but there was no point to it if it was true, as she had no intentions of staying here. And falling in love was *not* in her plan.

She tilted her head to one side, and a tendril of russet gold escaped the bonds of her neck and fell across his arm. Quickly she tossed it back into place.

No, love was not in her plan.

Ben stood at the post office the following Wednesday, sifting through the pile of mail that he received. He was waiting for a very important letter, but it was not there. Just a notice from the land office, a message from the regional church authority, and his copy of *Farmer's Weekly*.

He slapped the mail against his hand in frustration. How long would this letter take? He should have heard from his son by now.

He missed him. The house was too quiet now, too empty. Before the boy left, he'd been taking apart an old set of dresser drawers and hammering it back together so it was a sturdy, useful piece of furniture. It was something Ben himself had planned to do as a winter project, but the boy had been adamant about wanting to try it himself.

And what could it hurt? Nothing he could do to it would make it in worse shape than it was.

The pile of boards and carefully stacked nails were still waiting for Jacey in his bedroom, as were the toy metal plow and the pair of roller skates, which Ben had cleaned and oiled for him.

He had even crawled under the bed and moved the bureau to rescue all the stray marbles that had rolled around the room, and they were back in the leather bag by his son's bed. The child had a little boat that Ben had carved for him and a simple block locomotive that they were building together, and both were on the table in his room. A little toy cow watched the outside world from his window.

Everything was waiting for the boy's return.

"Nothing yet?" The postmaster came out from behind the bank of mailboxes and gave him a sympathetic look. Lionel Elderson was a gaunt, thin man with the biggest hands Ben had ever seen. Yet he could play the mandolin with an astonishing tenderness and delicacy.

"Not yet."

"When do you expect the boy home?" Lionel's large hands arranged the display of special envelopes and stamps and postcards on the counter. His wife, a champion china painter, had her wares on display there, too.

"I'd say three weeks, maybe even a month. It can't be too soon, I'll tell you."

The postmaster laughed. "It's strange, isn't it, how much you think you can't wait for just a little peace and quiet, and then you get some, and it's enough to break your heart. I know I was falling to pieces when little Leo spent a month with his cousins in Brookings, and Mabel and I thought our hearts couldn't stand all that silence. One night I told Mabel, 'Dear, you get out there in the yard and yell for a while and see if you can startle the chickens into not laying for a week, and I'll stand in the parlor and bounce a ball right next to the porcelain flowered lamp.'"

Ben chuckled. "I'm not quite at that point yet!"

Lionel motioned Ben to the side. "So," he said in a low voice, "word has it that you've brought someone to live here. Mail order?"

Ben stared at him, uncomprehending. "Mail-order what?"

"You know." Lionel wiggled his eyebrows. "Mail-order bride."

"Mail-order bride? What? Oh, Mariah! No! No! Absolutely not!"

Ben's objections were so vehement that others in

the post office turned to see what the fuss was about, and he dropped his voice. "No, Lionel, she's just staying in Karl and Lainie's house for a while, keeping it in shape for them until they get back."

He could tell Lionel wanted to ask more questions, but a line was starting to form at the service window, and he had to leave.

Ben watched him go back behind the wall of mailboxes and reappear at the window, and he thought about what the man had said.

Mail-order bride! What would they come up with next?

Perhaps the best idea was to introduce Mariah to the community. It would be a good idea for everyone, actually. Not only was it time for Prospect to meet Mariah, but it was also time for Mariah to meet Prospect.

For the next ten days, Mariah saw Ben only briefly each day. After settling her in with some food staples, food she suspected was from his own stores, he had stopped by to check on her and the livestock quickly and then left. Now that he had the plow part he'd needed, it was a race to get the crop in the ground in time.

Mariah found herself looking forward to his visits, however short they might be. It was loneliness, she knew, combined with a certain amount of boredom. The garden had been weeded, and now she was occupying her time sewing curtains for the kitchen window from a bright bolt of calico she'd brought with her.

Soon she'd have to go into town and meet this Meggin Sanders. The longer she delayed, the more time it would be until she found Joshua and returned him to civilization. She'd have to speak to Ben soon about riding to town with him the next time he went. This time of year, unfortunately, he spent most of his days in the fields.

Late in the morning, Ben pulled into her yard. He hopped off his wagon with a pleased expression on his face.

"Shut your eyes," he ordered, "and hold out your apron."

"What for?" She smiled as he fidgeted with excitement, like a young boy popping full of a secret.

"Just do it."

With an amused shrug, she complied. In moments, the skirt of her apron grew heavy.

"You can open your eyes now."

"Lemons!" The bright-yellow fruit filled her apron, and their fresh, clean scent tickled her nose. "But why—"

"Why lemons? So we can make lemonade, of course!" He went into her house, and she followed him, somewhat dazed by the bounty he'd given her.

Lemons! She couldn't have been more surprised if he had filled her apron with gold coins.

"Where did you get lemons?" she asked.

"In town, of course. Meggin Sanders just got in a shipment, and I was lucky enough to be Johnny-on-the-spot."

"Lemons in Prospect?"

He grinned. "Prospect may seem like the center of zero, but we're not as isolated here as you think."

He pulled an earthenware crock from the shelf and put it on the table. Then he handed her a knife. "Start squeezing!"

As she obeyed, reveling in the aroma of the lemon juice that covered her hands, he found the cone of sugar and began scraping it.

When he was through, he darted outside, lightning quick, pumped fresh water, and came back inside, where he dumped the water and the sugar in the crock.

With the big wooden spoon Mariah handed him, he stirred it. "Don't you want to wash your hands?" he asked when she stood by the table, her fingers splayed across her face.

"Absolutely not! This is better than the costliest perfume!"

"Oh really? This I've got to try!"

Ben took her hands and raised them to his face, and Mariah's breath caught in her throat.

His eyes looked directly into hers, and she was afraid that he could read there all the secrets etched onto her heart. For a breathless minute, she stared back into his eyes, wanting to read something there but finding herself only getting lost in the blue that was as endless as the Dakota skies.

She snatched back her hands and, like a little girl, hid them behind her back and said brightly, "Time to taste the lemonade."

He lifted the spoon to his lips and tasted the lemonade. "Think it needs more sugar?" he asked, holding the spoon toward her.

Mariah hesitated only a moment before leaning over and sipping from the spoon he offered.

"It's perfect," she sighed, and she had to remind herself that she was talking about the lemonade.

"Not quite yet," he responded, and before she could speak, he dashed out of the house again. Mariah moved toward the front door and watched him lift a burlap-wrapped package from his wagon and bring it inside.

He dropped it on the table, and the material fell away, revealing a chunk of ice.

"As I live and breathe," Mariah whispered. "Iced lemonade."

"Got some glasses we can use?" he asked as he chipped a bit off the square.

Mariah got two of the set of heavy cut-glass tumblers from the cupboard and handed them to Ben. Her mouth watered as she watched Ben splash the pale-yellow liquid over the clear crystalline chunks of ice.

Nothing had ever looked so inviting.

She took a drink of the lemonade and sighed happily. She could almost stand living in the Dakota Territory if there was iced lemonade at hand.

They took their drinks outside and sat in front of Mariah's doorway, letting the afternoon breeze cool their foreheads as they sipped the lemonade.

"How do you like it out here so far?" Ben's question was casual, but Mariah's answer was guarded.

"It's a new experience for me."

He tilted his chair against the outer wall of the

house. "When I came out here, I was torn between loving it and hating it. I loved the freedom the territory offered, and the chance to actually do something with my life. I hadn't had it so easy before."

"Where did you come from?" she asked, her fingers idly stroking the condensation from the side of the glass.

"Pennsylvania. My family owned a printing business, but my older brother took it over."

"He wouldn't let you work there?"

Ben's mouth curved wryly. "Oh, he let me work there, all right. But it wasn't long before he ran up more debts than he could pay, and before you could say Jack Robinson, we were bankrupt."

"Where is he now?"

Ben shrugged. "Somewhere in Pennsylvania, trying to make an easy buck."

Mariah feared she was prying, but she couldn't stop asking questions. "So why did you decide to come out here?"

"Olea—she's my sister, remember—and her husband heard about free land out here, so they talked me into coming west with them. And I'm mighty glad they did."

"But you said you hated it out here, too."

Ben brought his chair forward with a thump. "Sure. There's nothing easy in this life. Nothing at all. Farming is hard work, and there have been a couple of years when it's been touch and go. Seems sometimes like this land's dead set against a man making his way out here."

He took a deep breath and exhaled, and Mariah

could see him relax. "But then a day like today comes along, and you can't help but wonder if there's any other place on this earth that is as beautiful."

Mariah looked around her. A sea of green stretched to the horizon, broken only by an occasional line of trees. A cloud drifted lazily across the cerulean sky. The day was gloriously mild, and if she let herself, she could even see a spot of beauty in it.

But she quickly steeled herself against it. The only good thing here was her nephew, wherever he was, and as soon as she found him, she'd take that bit of light with her.

Ben turned his bright blue eyes on her. "So does this seem primitive to you?"

"Somewhat," she admitted, "though it's not as bad as I'd thought." It was a lie, but it was what Lorna would have called a social lie, done to move the conversation away from a dangerous area. She couldn't let the subject turn to her.

Actually, the only thing that wasn't as bad as she'd expected was the quiet. Not silence—there was entirely too much buzzing, cawing, and whinnying for the air to be entirely soundless—but the restful, low hum of nature at work. It was quite a change from the city's constant clanging and clamor, and it was a change that she had to admit, she preferred.

"Think you might stay awhile?" His voice was casual.

Mariah thought of Joshua. She didn't want him to live out here and learn to battle the land season after season, waiting only for the gentle days of June as respite. Joshua was destined for better things.

But she couldn't give him that answer. Instead, she said merely, "I don't suspect I will."

A wall sprang up between them, a wall named Dakota.

In an effort to dissolve the wall, she motioned toward the new curtains. "What do you think? Will Lainie like them?"

"I'm sure she will. I don't know anything about sewing, but it looks to me like you did a real nice job with those."

"Thank you," Mariah said. "I had to sew them by hand, so they took almost the whole afternoon. If I'd had a machine, I could have run them up in under an hour."

"You know how to use a sewing machine?"

Mariah nodded. "Certainly. That's what I used in Lowell."

"Then I can guarantee you a job with Meggin Sanders, as she's being run ragged with the demand for help. Right now she's only got old Mrs. Colby stitching for her, and she refuses to use the machine Meggin got from Minnesota. Says it's the Devil's apparatus."

Mariah laughed. "I've said that myself, when I've run a needle through my thumb."

He smiled, and Mariah relaxed, relieved that the wall had gone down again. "In that case, I've got the Devil's thresher, and his combine, and his plow, and a whole lot of small tools that belong to him, too."

Mariah faced him. "Why do you do it?" she asked,

suddenly serious. "Why do you go to war with the earth every day of your life?"

Ben wiped a line down the edge of his now-empty glass. "That's a good question. I suppose I do it because I believe in it."

He dug his heel into the ground and scraped it back and forth. Then he reached down and scooped up a handful of dirt. "See this?" A trickle of black dirt ran out of his fist. "This is the best soil in the world. Valley soil. Dark and rich and full of everything a plant needs to grow out here."

"But plants grow nearly everywhere," she protested. "Why come out here?"

He motioned around him. "Just like the soil is filled with everything a plant needs, the air is filled with everything a child needs. It's a good place for a boy to grow up."

"A boy?" Mariah's throat constricted. Had he discovered her search?

A proud smile split Ben's face. "I've got the best son a man could ask for. He's six years old, a mite small for his age, but coming along just great. He's going to be a swell farmer someday, just like his dad."

"A son?" Mariah's confusion was overwhelming. "I didn't know you had a son. Where is he?"

"He's in St. Paul right now with his buddy Bo and his family. They had a big family wedding to go to, and they offered to have Jacey come along to keep Bo company. It's a long trip, after all, and a bit of a trial for a little boy. It's nice to have some way to keep Bo occupied." He grinned. "Bo is a bit of a whirlwind.

Travelling with him must be interesting. Anyway, they should be back in three or four weeks. They're also going to do some sightseeing while they're out there. I sure do miss him."

Mariah hadn't known about a son. If he had a child, then surely he had a wife. She scolded herself against the jealousy that rose unexpectedly in her chest. What did she care if he had a wife and a whole parcel of children?

She struggled with this new knowledge—and the feelings that it created in her. Why wouldn't he have told her he had a wife? A touch of contrariness bubbled up inside her. She'd address the issue head-on. She sat up straight in her chair. "I do get a mite lonesome out here sometimes," she said stiffly. "Perhaps you could introduce me to your wife."

"I've been widowed for some time now."

"Oh, I'm sorry." Mariah's voice was meek.

Ben pondered her face for a moment before speaking. "It was a marriage arranged by my brother in a futile attempt to rescue the business."

"Oh." She knew she was frowning. An arranged marriage?

His words were blunt, and his face closed with obvious pain. "She was the daughter of Alton Covington." Ben's blue eyes flashed to her face, and Mariah was shocked at the anger she saw there. "Name mean anything to you?"

"No."

"Alton Covington owned several large paper mills, some as far away as Michigan. Sam, my brother, saw an opportunity to mingle two obviously compatible businesses, printing and paper production, while salvaging the Harris name, which had come to be synonymous with unpaid bills." His voice was hard with bitterness. "He thought that if the two families merged through marriage, corporate bonding would soon follow."

"Why didn't *he* marry her?"

Ben barked a short laugh. "Oh, I'm sure he thought about it. Unfortunately, he was already somewhat inconveniently married. I don't doubt that he considered divorce, but the Covingtons, staunch Catholics that they are, would never have allowed Cecelia to marry a divorced man."

"But how does anyone arrange a marriage nowadays? Especially when, well—" Mariah struggled for the words to phrase the question delicately. "What I mean is that if your company had a somewhat unsavory reputation, and Covington's business was…" She let the sentence fade.

"I know what you're asking. I'm not really sure myself how it happened. Sam was a master of deception. He got us invited to the finest houses in Scranton and managed to get us in the whirl of elite society. It's amazing how the rich excuse the rich, even though we were only a lawsuit away from the poorhouse."

"So they believed you were wealthy."

"Yes. And that made the marriage possible. I don't think the Covingtons normally marry out of their social caste."

"You must have loved her," Mariah said quietly.

"No, I don't think I did," he responded, his voice thoughtful. "My head was in the clouds, right where Sam had planted it. I don't think I was capable of falling in love."

He toyed with his empty lemonade glass. "Anyway, the scheme came to a crashing halt when Cecelia died in childbirth. All the plans that Sam had made fell through as the Covingtons pulled out of Pennsylvania, away from the memories of their daughter."

"I'm so sorry," Mariah whispered.

Ben sat up straight, as if shaking off the past. "Well, that's probably more than you wanted to hear," he said briskly. "The story of how Harris and Sons went belly-up and I lost my wife. Not a pretty story, nor one that I'm proud of."

"But you have your son," Mariah said softly.

"Yes, and Jacey is everything to me. I can't wait for you to meet him. He's a fine boy."

Joshua was only a year younger than Jacey, Mariah thought. Her mind toyed with the vision of the two boys playing together, but she promptly erased any notion of that from her mind. As soon as she found Joshua, they were leaving. And Jacey would have to play by himself.

The best thing to do was to move on to a safer topic. Thankfully, Ben stepped up.

"I was wondering," he said, clearing his throat, "if you'd be interested in going to church services with me tomorrow. Afterward we're having a special dinner, and it would be a good chance for you to meet the other people of Prospect."

"A dinner?" She stood up, the lemonade temporarily forgotten. "I'd love to go! Is it a covered-dish dinner? Should I bring anything?"

"You don't have to bring anything except yourself. I'll introduce you to the members of the church. Almost everybody in Prospect goes to First."

"First?" she asked blankly.

"That's the name of the church. We like to joke that the full name is First and Only since there isn't another church for at least twenty miles. We'll have a service, too, with Reverend Timms, who is a bang-up preacher."

The idea of meeting the residents of Prospect all at once was both daunting and exciting. She'd have the chance to gently inquire if any of them had seen Joshua.

How would she do that though? She couldn't just ask and risk the door slamming shut. She'd have to be cautious about what she said and what she asked.

One thing she would not do is lie. "Not only are lies a trap that we use to capture our own failings," Lorna used to tell her over and over, "but they are an affront to God."

So she'd go to the dinner and listen, and let her eyes and ears learn what they could.

And the church service itself was going to be like swimming in the River Jordan. Refreshing to the soul!

First lemonade—iced lemonade—and now church! What a great day!

* * *

The soft clopping of the horse's hooves was the only sound breaking the silence of the afternoon as Ben rode home. He let the reins lie slack in his hands as he thought about the afternoon.

How had it turned like that? It had started so gaily with the lemons and had quickly changed to solemn.

He hadn't intended for the conversation to become so personal, but something about Mariah drew him out. He hadn't talked about Cecelia—or even thought about her—for months. It still bothered him that he hadn't felt more than a passing sadness at her death. And yet there was still a part of him that kept those emotions locked away, for his brother's trickery and Cecelia's death had more to do with each other than he'd admitted.

It had been Sam's baby she was carrying when she died.

Chapter 3

Ben picked her up on Sunday morning, and they rode together into Prospect, Old Gray pulling the wagon in a practiced path.

Mariah could barely contain her excitement. Maybe one of these folks would be the key to finding Joshua, and the chance to worship with others was an added goodness.

She even wore her new shoes, ones that she had purchased before going to New York. They were impractical things, made of a nearly sheer leather that wouldn't last more than a few wearings, and on the end of each lacing was a tassel of shiny green, thick cording. The toes came to a sharp point, covered with a tracery of silvered metal.

She'd splurged on them, expecting to enjoy a good

laugh with Lorna over the outrageous style. She and her sister had always worn the same sized shoe, and she had envisioned them parading around the apartment, pretending they were fine ladies out for a stroll.

Now, though, they were getting their maiden voyage on Dakota dirt.

She had chosen to wear them today to bolster her confidence, and to remind her what her job was here—to find Joshua.

She peeped down to look at them. They *were* beautiful shoes, though. She clicked the toes together just to hear the sound of the metal tips. Maybe she was vain, but she really did like them.

Her stomach was all butterflies and grasshoppers by the time Ben pulled up next to the church. It was, like the other buildings in the small town, recently built, but the townspeople's faith was evident in the way the church was painted white, and bright flowers, mostly daisies and irises, bloomed in cultivated beds around the outside of it.

Two lilac bushes stood on either side of the door, fully in bloom. She breathed in the scent, filling her lungs with the soft sweetness of the pale-purple blossoms. Had there ever been such a delightful aroma?

She determined that when Lainie and Karl and their new baby arrived at their home again, lilac bushes would surround them. It would be her gift to them.

Ben held his arms up and swung her down from the wagon. As her feet touched the ground, her toe caught on a tuft of grass, and the sharp end of the shoe dislodged the clod of dirt and roots, and she looked up at him as she stumbled a bit. Those incredibly sky-colored eyes were lit with laughter as he caught her before she righted herself.

"Are you all right?" he asked.

"I am. I'm just excited to be here."

"Those are some city shoes, that's for sure," he said. "I can't say that I've seen anything like them on the women's feet here."

She bit her lip. Maybe she shouldn't have worn them. Would they make her seem as if she was putting on airs?

Maybe she was. And here she was, going into church. She tugged her skirt down in an attempt to cover the shoes.

Ben tucked his Bible in one hand and guided her by her elbow with his other toward the church door, where a small group of people had gathered. He walked slowly, probably, she thought, in deference to the shoes, afraid that if she were left to her own devices, she'd fall face-first into a cluster of irises.

The people stopped talking and turned to her. She expected them to gawk at her, but instead their faces were warm with smiles, and two of the women stepped forward.

"Welcome to First!" one said cordially, extending her hand. "I'm Olea Martlett, Ben's sister." Her round face, wreathed by a braid of light-brown hair, beamed.

"And I'm Andrea Timms," the other said. Her eyes were as dark as her hair and sparkled with vitality. "My husband is the minister here, and I am the organist."

The others stepped forward to introduce themselves,

and more came out of the front of the church to greet
her. It was a whirl of names and faces, and Mariah
knew she'd never remember who was who—at least
not today.

Ben guided her to the second row. Instead of the
dark walnut pews of the church Mariah had attended
as a child, the seats were made of carefully sanded
light wood. Sunlight flooded the sanctuary through
the windows on each side of the room. The windows
were open, and the gentle breeze of a summer morning kept the air moving throughout.

Andrea Timms took her place at the organ. It was
a small, parlor-sized instrument, but it was ideal for
the size of the sanctuary. She began to play, moving
from one familiar hymn to another as the congregation filed in and took their places.

Mariah studied the interior of the church. The altar
was a simple arrangement, a plain oaken table with a
white cloth cover. But over it was something that took
her by surprise.

It was a complete tableau of scenes from the Bible,
painted in glowing colors with great skill as a triptych.
She saw Adam and Eve in the Garden of Eden, Noah
on the ark with the animals, and Moses parting the Red
Sea on one panel. On the second was the Annunciation
of Mary, the Magi travelling across the desert, and the
angels over the stable where Jesus lay in a manger with
Joseph, Mary, and the shepherds nearby. On the third
was the Crucifixion, Jesus' appearance to Mary, and
His ascension into heaven.

The artistry was astonishing.

She nudged Ben and whispered, "That's really beautiful!"

He bent toward her and spoke in a low voice. "It was painted by an early resident of Prospect, a saint who's gone on to be with the Lord. We're quite blessed to have this as a memory of him. He passed on two years ago. Can you believe he painted that when he was in his eighties?"

She shook her head, almost disbelieving him. The colors and style were so true, the painting might have easily been mistaken for the work of a Renaissance artist whose works hung in the finest museums.

Reverend Timms stepped up to the podium and invited them to stand for the beginning hymn, "Rock of Ages."

Ben reached for the hymnal in the rack in front of them, and, after looking at the sign on the slate at the front of the church where the hymn numbers were written, located the correct page.

They shared the hymnal, and as she sang along with Ben's true tenor, she thought about how much she had missed going to church. For the past three years, she had been so intent on saving money by working two jobs that she had been too exhausted on Sunday mornings to go to church.

Had it told in her soul? It seemed like it. Each note of the beloved hymn cleaned a bit of the accumulated grime from her soul, and she felt immensely better as the verses progressed.

"Today's Bible verse," Reverend Timms said, "is

from the book of Ruth. Let's look at it. Chapter two, please, verse twenty."

Ben opened his Bible and found the spot. He held it so that she could follow along.

"'Blessed be he of the Lord, who hath not left off his kindness to the living and to the dead.'" Reverend Timms paused. "Let's read that again. 'Blessed be he of the Lord, who hath not left off his kindness to the living and to the dead.' The living and to the dead. What does that mean?"

Mariah held her breath. Where was the sermon headed? If it involved talking about a loved one dying, she didn't know if she could make it through without crying.

"Let's look at the story of Ruth, which begins, really, by being the story of Naomi. Naomi's life is difficult. She loses her husband and her sons. Everyone but her two daughters-in-law, Orpah and Ruth."

Mariah nodded slightly. She knew this story.

"Naomi releases Orpah and Ruth, but Ruth stays with her, with the famous words: 'Intreat me not to leave thee, or to return from following after thee: for whither thou goest, I will go; and where thou lodgest, I will lodge: thy people shall be my people, and thy God my God: Where thou diest, will I die, and there will I be buried: the Lord do so to me, and more also, if ought but death part thee and me.' Let's read those words out loud together."

Mariah barely trusted her voice at first, but buoyed by Ben's strong voice, she joined in and read along.

"If we take Ruth's words apart, she is promising to

stay with Naomi for the rest of her life—for Naomi's life and for Ruth's. She will be buried with Naomi. That's a love that transcends what we usually think of between a mother and her daughter-in-law. They weren't even related to each other except through what we must assume was a wonderfully successful marriage between Ruth and Naomi's son."

He paused and turned to smile at his wife. "And how else would Naomi's son have come to have such a good marriage except by seeing his own parents'? We tend to give the credit entirely to Ruth for this steadfastness, but we need to consider that Naomi must have been an extraordinary woman and an incredible mother and a loving wife. We are lucky if we have anyone like her in our lives. I know I am."

Andrea Timms's face glowed with joy at the recognition.

"The other part of this story that we often overlook is what drove Naomi and Ruth to Bethlehem. It was famine." He leaned on the podium and spoke intently. "I cannot imagine anything worse than watching someone I love slowly starve to death. When Ruth insisted on going with Naomi on this trip, she was making sure that her mother-in-law would live. And that's what drives the rest of the story, to her gleaning from Boaz's fields, and to their own eventual love story."

The minister looked at his open Bible. "Notice, too, that Boaz has a part to play in this story. He makes sure that Ruth's work is enabled. This is one of the nicest parts of this story. He lets Ruth do what Ruth needs to do. He has respect for her and for what she has to do. When Ruth tells Naomi whose fields she's been gleaning in, that's when Naomi speaks the words that form our verse for today. Let's read this one together, please."

Mariah read with the others: " 'Blessed be he of the Lord, who hath not left off his kindness to the living and to the dead.' "

"Naomi gives her blessing," he said, looking up at the congregation, "and there are two ways to read this line. Is it Boaz who is kind to the living and the dead? Or does Naomi mean God? Or, is it possible—and I think it is—to see it in a broader context, that it can be read both ways, and perhaps we should? It's something I'd like you all to think about this week as we go through our daily lives. Is our kindness the kindness of the Lord? Can we make ourselves more like Him, in everything we do? I think we can.

"Additionally," he continued, "I'd like you to consider how we give kindness to the dead. There are many ways we can do this. We can respect their wishes. We can acknowledge their contribution, such as our departed brother who painted this glorious backdrop to the altar. We can do our utmost to make sure that their lives are, even after death, not forgotten. There are undoubtedly other ways we can celebrate with kindness."

He beamed at them. "And now, with one last song, we will dismiss to the side room of the church, where you may, in ways Ruth never dreamed of, glean to your heart's content in the dinner that the Ladies' Aid has set up."

The parting song was "Bringing in the Sheaves." The words came back to Mariah with ease.

As the church members stood and began to make their way to the side room for dinner, more of them introduced themselves to Mariah.

It surprised her how comfortable she felt, even with the casual exchanges about the beautiful weather, the progression of the crops, the kittens that had been born behind the post office, and so on.

Then Ben led her into the room where dinner was being served.

She had never seen such a lavish display. Hams covered in a dark sugar glaze. Roast beef sliced thick with fluffy mounds of potatoes at the side. Carrots swimming in golden butter. Beans topped with slices of bacon. Yeasty rolls in puffy piles. Cakes as high as hatboxes.

Her mouth began to water as the vision of the laden table promised a delicious meal. As soon as she sat down, a filled plate appeared in front of her courtesy of an apron-swathed woman who announced, "Here you are, dearie," and she dug in.

A cloud of conversation mingled with the aromatic drift from the food in front of her. As she savored the tender ham and savory carrots, words separated from the discussions around her.

Wheat is looking good...early harvest...buy a new plow maybe...

Baby...growing like a weed...baptism next month...

Calving at the Halvorson's...thinking of adding...

She heard them only vaguely, concentrating as she

was on her meal. Ben was deep in discussion with the fellow next to him, and she caught wisps of what they were talking about. Apparently the guy next to him, a large, ruddy-faced gentleman whose name might have been Lars, but she wasn't sure, was telling Ben about some dogs he had seen.

Dishes were being passed around the table, and Mariah found herself scooping roast beef and spoonfuls of creamy mashed potatoes and green beans and more dinner rolls onto her plate. It was all so good.

The conversation about the dogs went on without her contribution to it as she devoted herself to enjoying her food.

Puppies in the barn...mongrels, but so sweet...your boy should...

Dogs. Big things that barked loudly and smelled odd. That's what she thought of them. Give her a nice soft kitten any day, especially one that was worth its weight in mice.

Ben responded to the man. "I think we'll get a cat. With all that wheat nearby, we've got more mice in the area than mosquitoes, and that's saying something."

Was he reading her mind?

When she got Joshua, she would take him back to the East Coast with her and let him have whatever pets he wanted—within limits. Lorna had written her a letter once, telling her that the boy had started his own zoo in the apartment. Mariah had smiled until she read further. Lorna had told her what he'd found in the apartment and on the street to stock his "zoo," and her vow to get them out of the tenement had strengthened.

Wherever he was now, she hoped the family had some kind of pet for the boy.

"And maybe a dog, too," he added. "If I know Jacey, though, he'll have the house filled with cats and dogs and gophers and snakes. The kid has the kindest heart ever. We'll have a menagerie of critters for sure."

Ben's son and Joshua were so much alike. Only a year apart, they might have been friends. Her heart soared with hope. Maybe they *were* friends. She could barely wait to meet the little boy and find out.

Her thoughts were interrupted when Olea, Ben's sister, came up behind her, leaned over her shoulder, and asked, "Would you like a dessert? We have apple pie, gooseberry pie, blackberry pie, blueberry pie, white cake, brown sugar tarts, fruitcake slices, strawberry shortcake, and vanilla cookies. I'm sorry, but we're out of sugared *lefse*, and am I ever hearing about *that*."

She wanted to laugh. She'd lost track of what the offerings were. There were so many, and she had no idea what lefse was, but honestly, how could someone not find something else to like in that list!

"I'll have some of that white cake, please." She motioned Olea a bit closer. "What, by the way, is *lefse*, and why are people so upset about it?"

"It's a Norwegian treat, kind of a flat bread made from potatoes and served spread with butter and sprinkled with sugar."

"I see," Mariah said, although of course she didn't. Bread sprinkled with sugar?

Within minutes Olea was back with a slice of the white cake that extended over the edge of the dessert plate. Mariah wanted to protest that she couldn't eat that much, but she was in a church and not about to begin lying. She knew she would eat every scrumptious bite.

"By the way," Olea whispered in her ear, "those are the most beautiful shoes I've ever seen in my life. I think I'll dream about them tonight."

Mariah smiled, but the truth was that the stunning shoes pinched and rubbed and chafed, and the second she got back to the small house, she was going to get out of them and hide them under the bed.

She shoved the thought aside and focused on the cake. It tasted just as good as it looked, and she realized with embarrassment that she had eaten in that single meal more than she had consumed in the past three days.

At last the plates were cleared, the coffee served, and those gathered began to leave for home. She rose to her feet, hobbled painfully to the kitchen area, and offered to help with the cleanup, but Andrea Timms told her that it was all taken care of and she could help out the next time.

The next time. She didn't comment.

Instead, she balanced against the wall, trying to move inconspicuously from foot to foot, and tried a beginning entry into a conversation she hoped would lead to information about Joshua. If anyone knew about the area and children, it would probably be the minister's wife.

"How many families attend First?" she asked, hoping she sounded casual and didn't look too idiotic as she teetered back and forth on her aching feet, trying to give each one even a moment's respite.

"Anywhere between forty and fifty," Andrea said. "Of course, that doesn't mean they all come usually. We have a lot today because of the dinner."

"I suppose many of them have children." Even as she said it, she knew it sounded really bad, but surprisingly, the minister's wife didn't seem to notice.

"They do."

"It must make life easier on the farm."

"I'm sure it does. Say, could you hand me that gravy boat?"

Fortunately the dish was close enough and didn't require her to walk to get it, and she stretched across and retrieved it and gave it back to Andrea.

Mariah was about to ask about those families without children, but at that moment Ben came back in. "I think we should think about going. It looks like it's going to rain."

Rain? She limped to the window. The sky, which had been so clear before, was now spotted with occasional clouds.

"See that?" he asked, coming up behind her. "That's the west. Weather comes from the west out here. And that big dark spot that's looming on the horizon? It's far away, but it'll get here soon enough, and maybe it'll wear itself out before it arrives and we'll get nothing, or maybe it'll gather momentum—and moisture— and we'll be drenched. But I'll be honest, I don't like what I see."

Within minutes, they had expressed their appreciation to the Ladies' Aid group and were headed back to their homes.

Old Gray must have sensed some urgency, perhaps transmitted through the reins, or perhaps from a sheer animal sense of understanding the weather, and he trotted along quickly.

"I hope you don't mind that we cleared out so quickly," Ben said. "After that tornado in Grand Forks last month, I'm a bit weather-shy."

She sat up. "Tornado? Where's Grand Forks?"

"Grand Forks is about seventy-five miles north of Fargo. On June 17, a bad tornado tore through there. Five people died, and many more were injured. A church was destroyed, and part of the university, too."

She hugged her arms to herself nervously. "I suppose you get a lot of tornadoes here."

"No more than anywhere else."

She wasn't sure about that. Even one tornado was too many.

"I can see that this isn't going to be a tornado. Not even a thunderstorm," he said reassuringly. "Just a nice, steady rain. You'll be fine."

Great plops of rain had just started when they arrived at Mariah's new home, and she waved him on as she tore inside.

She headed for the first available chair and crossed her right ankle over her left knee and undid the shoe. Then she reversed the action for the left shoe.

Her feet screamed in pain as she took them out of the shoes, and she sighed as she saw the blisters the fashionable footwear had caused.

"Never again," she said to them, sadly relegating the green tassels and metal filigree toes to under her bed. "The next shoes I buy may not be right out of *Godey's*, but I honestly don't care."

She leaned back in the chair, her feet finally free of the offending shoes, and let herself melt into the cushions. How long had it been since she had been this relaxed, this content? It was a question she couldn't really answer. It had been too long ago.

There had been something relaxing about the day. It was partly the church service, partly the cordiality of the church members, partly the dinner.

Something joggled her musing. *Could it be, maybe, just a little bit perhaps, the land? The openness of the prairie, the sky that overarched the endless land? The sense that nothing could touch her, emotionally or physically, as long as this space was around her? It was the same sun, the same sky, the same earth as it had been in Massachusetts, but here—it was different.*

No, that couldn't be it. She was not impressed with this place. There was nothing in it, nothing at all. When she left—with Joshua—Dakota would be as empty as it could be. Nothing of value would be there.

Nothing except Ben.

Ben hammered at the plow. The recalcitrant bolt was still giving him trouble, but he couldn't risk breaking it, not at this point in the season, so he had to keep his wits about him.

It was amazing how something as little, as seem-

ingly unimportant, as a circlet of metal could throw a
man's plans into chaos.

Or a woman.

His experience with women was limited. Actually,
it was experience with *a* woman. Cecelia. She had
spoiled him from ever loving a woman again.

He smacked the bolt with a bit too much enthusi-
asm, and a little chip of metal broke off.

"Sorry," he said to the bolt—or the universe, perhaps. "I got a little bit carried away."

That's what women did to a man. They made him
do stupid, stupid things, like nearly break a bolt, and
then apologize to it.

Or fall in love with her.

He wasn't going to fall in love with Mariah. He had
to focus on his son for a while, give him the best life,
the most supporting love, he possibly could.

God had blessed him so richly. It wasn't good for
him to focus on the past, to think about Cecelia and
what she had done. What he needed to do was consider
the godsends—and do so in gratitude.

Like this land, which spoke to his soul and which
supported his life.

Like Jacey, who gave him what he thought he could
never know.

And maybe like Mariah, who made him think of
loving again.

A few days later Ben appeared at Mariah's door and
announced, "Let's take you to see Prospect. You've

seen the church, and now I think it's time you visited the town itself."

Mariah flew to the mirror, her hands fluttering around her head like small birds. "Ben Harris, you could give a body some advance notice, you know."

"For what? For going into town?" He leaned against the doorjamb and eyed her curiously. "I have to admit, Mariah, this surprises me. I didn't think you'd be so excited about going into Prospect."

Her hands stopped; the birds came to rest as she considered his words. Why on earth was she so excited about going into Prospect? It wasn't, after all, like it was New York City or Boston. She knew what she was going to find: a little, moth-eaten hole in the edge of eternity.

She stared at her reflection in the mirror.

Why, she asked herself again, why did she worry about whether her hair was in order? If her dress was unwrinkled? If there was a streak of dirt across her cheek, which there was, so she scrubbed at it furiously.

Certainly she didn't care what people in Prospect thought of her.

But she did, she reminded herself. These people might hold the key to finding Joshua, and that was the best reason of all.

And a little corner of her mind niggled at her: *You care what Ben thinks.*

Mariah straightened her back and firmed her resolve. She didn't care about the people in Prospect, she didn't care about her appearance, and she certainly didn't care about Ben.

So there, she said to her reflected image. *Now go into town and find Joshua. The sooner you can do that, the sooner you'll be out of this dusty place and back in the cradle of civilization.*

And away from Ben? the little voice persisted.

She ignored it. Yes, she ignored it.

The trip into town passed quickly, and soon she saw the small dot on the horizon that was Prospect.

She squinted, trying to see it without his knowing she cared. But as they neared, she found herself scooting closer to the edge of her seat.

Her stomach roiled with anxiety. Perhaps here she would get clues to Joshua's whereabouts. If only that was so, she prayed silently. She wanted to hug him so much that her arms ached with emptiness.

But there was another reason for her trepidation.

She was eager to see another human being again.

The thought startled her. It had been fantastic to go to church and see people, but they were people who knew each other, who already had histories together. They all seemed to be friends. One thing she didn't want to do was make friends out here on the prairie. Friends complicated things. Friends tied you down. Friends made you tell secrets.

Oh, how she missed having a friend.

Already Ben had taken on epic proportions in her mind. He was special to her in ways that she had never wanted. He had become a friend.

And it wasn't that she doubted that. She just needed a woman to talk to, although she had no idea what she'd say. She had to be so guarded with her words and actions. Maybe friendship was too difficult right now.

The dots on the horizon became squares, and then rectangles, and soon they took on the recognizable shapes of buildings. There weren't many of them, but it was clearly a little community.

Ben pointed at the trees in the back of the church as they drove past. "By the way, that grove of trees behind it is natural. Nobody had to plant them—it's not a tree claim or anything like that—and the reason they grow so well there is because there's water back there. It's probably not grand enough to call it a river, but we do. It's called Little Dog River after the prairie dog villages you'll find further downstream."

She craned her head to see the river, but she couldn't make it out through the trees.

They headed into the center of the town.

Prospect was quite a bit different from Fargo, Mariah thought as she looked down the main street of the small town. While Fargo had boasted several large stores and hotels, Prospect had to content itself with Sanders Mercantile, the only business Mariah could see.

She nearly sprang from the wagon. Only decorum prevented her from sprinting into the store, especially when a bolt of bright-blue material in the store window caught her attention.

But she waited for Ben to get down first and come around to help her step from the buckboard. Almost absently, she let him hold her hand as she disembarked.

Her thoughts left the cloth and funneled onto his

hands. Warm and strong, whether holding the reins or calming Old Gray, cutting lemons or shaving the cone of sugar, they had quickly become symbols of steadfastness and reliability.

Oh, stop it! she scolded herself. *They're hands, nothing special. You could probably find them on anyone out here.*

"You're smiling." Ben's voice broke into her thoughts.

"Sometimes I do amuse myself," she replied.

He waited, expecting more from her, so she tried to explain. "I was having a little talk with myself that got very philosophical before it turned totally absurd."

"I see," he said slowly. "And what were you talking to yourself about?"

"Um—" Her eyes darted to quickly scan his face. "I was thinking about you."

He stopped. "And which was I, philosophical or absurd?"

"It's possible to be both at the same time," she said, busily straightening her skirt and not meeting his gaze.

He took her hand and helped her over the store's threshold. "And furthermore," he said as he leaned close enough for his breath to stir her hair, "what were you thinking about me?"

"Maybe that was the absurd part," she said out of the corner of her mouth.

She stood stock-still at the door of Meggin's store. After spending the ride into town in the brilliant June sunshine, she had to pause to let her eyes adjust to the comparative darkness of the store's interior.

Bit by bit, it came into focus. She would never have guessed there would be a place like this on the prairie. Every nook and cranny was occupied by something. Not a single bit of space had gone unutilized, and yet the entire store was neat.

She was drawn to the fabric section, which was set against the far corner, probably to avoid any chance of sun damage and fading.

What she saw astonished her.

Bolt after bolt of material was propped against a wall, and she walked over to it. It was arranged in an orderly rainbow, from deep violet all the way through vivid reds and bright yellows and every color in between. Next to them were spools and spools of thread, also tidily set in order, and boxes of lace, mostly white but with some ivory and black included, were set in piles according to color and width and texture. She trailed her fingers through the button cards, which were set in a clever wire stand beside the threads.

A heavy-set woman stepped from behind the counter and waved to Ben as he slipped out of the store. The woman wiped her hands on the voluminous white apron that enfolded her pillow of a chest. "You must be Mariah Rose," she boomed, her eyes as dark as two raisins set in unbaked dough, unabashedly taking stock of Mariah's appearance.

Mariah automatically smoothed the front of her dress. "Yes, I am. Are you by any chance Meggin Sanders?"

"One and the same." Meggin pumped Mariah's arm in a hearty handshake, as if Mariah were a rusty water pump needing to be primed. "Say, Ben Harris tells me you can turn a good stitch."

Torn between modesty and the need to get the work, Mariah nodded. "I was the head finisher at Linford Mills in Lowell, Massachusetts. I also worked at the sample shop next door to it."

"Now, doesn't that sound nice? 'Course, I don't know anything about mills back East. You make this dress?" Meggin reached out and turned back the cuff on Mariah's sleeve with a pudgy hand. "Hmmm, nice work. Can barely see the stitches."

"Thank you."

"How are you at buttonholes?"

"Better than most. I did the ones on this dress. Here, take another look at the sleeve. See those? What do you think?"

Mariah tried not to swell with pride as Meggin examined the buttonholes. She'd had to do so many at the mill that she'd quickly developed the knack of getting them done quickly and efficiently—and, most important, flawlessly. Only one other woman there was employed as a seamstress, and her buttonholes were uneven and wrinkled and frayed.

"So you won't balk at buttonholes?" Meggin persisted.

"I do my work, and I do it well," Mariah answered, her chin up. "You'd have to go a fair distance to find anyone better than I at sewing. I don't say it to brag. I say it as fact of the matter. God gave me this talent, and I have developed it as much as I am able."

"How about seams and hems? I don't like a hem that can be seen."

"If you'd like to step into a back area, I can show you my seams and my hems. All of my hems are sewn as invisible hems, catching only a thread and smoothed and pulled continually as I work around the border."

"Collars?"

"Collars require special handling if they're to be starched and worn with stays. If not, there's no difference in that part of a garment and another."

The store woman nodded. "We don't do fancy dress shirts here—no call for it, to tell the truth—but if the demand did arise, could you sew them?"

"Absolutely," Mariah said, confident in her skills.

Meggin rocked back on her heels and eyed Mariah with a frankly appraising gaze. "Well, young lady, sure looks like you know how to put a needle to cloth. If you want the work, I'd be right glad for the help." She named a wage only slightly less than Mariah had made in Lowell.

With the exchange of a bundle of material and a handshake, Mariah Rose became gainfully employed in the Dakota Territory.

Mariah was waiting at the wagon for Ben. "Look!" she said excitedly. "Meggin Sanders gave me thirty shirts to sew! Of course, some of them are partially finished. And oddly, they all have the same part left to take care of." She leaned over and said in a conspiratorial whisper, "Seems old Mrs. Colby thinks buttonholes are the Devil's device, too."

* * *

Her fingers fairly flew into the package when she got home, so eager was she to start. Ben called good-bye to her, and she waved over her shoulder at him.

The cloth was evenly woven, quality yard goods. It was actually much better than the material she had often handled at the mill.

She explored the rest of the package. There was a new packet of needles, precious, she knew, here on the prairie. Even in the mill, seamstresses guarded their needles. Every one of them had a favorite one, a needle that would slip through cloth like light through air. Her own was worn so thin that every time she used it, she was afraid it would break.

These needles she would use on basic sewing, such as long seams, to begin the process of wearing them down a bit. A new needle felt odd when she was doing delicate work. She liked them a bit worn in the middle, so she could feel the resistance of the cloth against the needle as she sewed. It warned her about the weave of the material, and of any problems with the thread itself.

But where was the thread? She tore into the wrappings, checked under the chair to see if it had rolled there, stood up and brushed out the fold of her dress. No thread.

Luckily she had some left after sewing the curtains. But it wouldn't last long. She'd have to go into Prospect.

She hummed as she smoothed out the material Meggin had given her. A few quick snips of her scissors, and there were the parts of a collar. Pieces that would be sleeves took their place. Cuffs. Shirt fronts. Soon the yardage became recognizable as shirts.

Or parts of shirts. Until she had more thread, she'd have to plan carefully how to use what she had. Buttonholes would have to wait, she thought with gratitude. Old Mrs. Colby wasn't totally alone in her opinion of buttonholes.

Mariah reached for the pincushion she'd brought with her from Massachusetts. She could at least pin the shirts together.

As she positioned the parts and pinned them into place, her mind drifted back to the afternoon. She realized that the day seemed wrapped in golden sunshine. That she had enjoyed herself. That she had been with people she liked, Ben and Meggin.

That she was actually having a good time in Dakota.

It couldn't be. It wasn't possible. Faster she worked, furiously pinning the shirt pieces together. Anything to remove the horrid thought from her mind.

A sudden jab reminded her to pay attention to her work. Automatically she put her finger in her mouth before the blood could stain the white cloth.

Like Dakota? Like Ben?

She shuddered, but it was a halfhearted shudder.

She took her finger out of her mouth. It wasn't bleeding, so she carefully picked up the last shirt she'd assembled.

A cuff was pinned to the center of the front panel. A collar piece was attached to the shirt tail. And a pocket adorned the neck.

She'd have to do something. Think about something

else, anything to get her mind off stupid Dakota, stupid Ben, and back on her purpose here: to find Joshua.

She sank onto the chair. For the first time, she allowed herself to think the impossible: what if she couldn't find him?

The sun set as Mariah sat in the darkening room, thinking. There had to be some way to start trying to find him. Every day she waited, his trail got colder. But what could she do?

And by the time the last ray of light had disappeared, she'd come up with a solution.

Ben stood outside the barn, glaring at the cultivator. He needed to get into the field today. It was a perfect day for farming, not overly cold nor hot, and dry with no rain in sight. What he really wanted to do today was cultivate because the weeds needed to be dealt with.

He hadn't even gotten the thing out of the barn, and one of the wheels had fallen off.

"You know," he said aloud to Old Gray, who watched the goings-on with only faint interest, "if we farmers had a shiny penny for each time some piece of machinery broke down and delayed us somehow, we'd be in the most remunerative business in the world."

He rubbed his chin and walked around the broken implement. He was a calm man, but there were times when farming was the most frustrating thing a person could do.

He could fix this. He knelt beside it and looked at the wheel and the rest of the cultivator. Once again, it was a bolt of some kind.

He walked back into the barn and looked in the area where the machine had been stored. There wasn't a bolt there that he could see, but just to make sure, he got on his hands and knees in the half-light of the open door and crawled the entire area, feeling with his hands in case it blended in too well with the shadows.

No luck.

Well, this put a different shine on the day. Without the bolt, the cultivator wouldn't work. Without the cultivator, the weeds would take over. With the weeds winning, the wheat would suffer.

And he didn't have the time to wait for another one to be shipped from Minneapolis.

He rocked back on his heels and thought. He could, he reasoned, see if he could get the bolt from Meggin, although the last time that hadn't worked out at all well. Maybe he could take a trip to Fargo? Again, the last time, they hadn't had the part he needed.

Another farmer might have it, but he didn't really have time to go farm to farm to see if anyone had a spare bolt.

Could he borrow a cultivator? He shook his head even as he thought it. Of course his neighbors would come through for him and, at their own expense, lend him what he needed, but the truth was that they each needed to be using the cultivator themselves.

Maybe he could rig up something. He wasn't the best mechanic in the world, but maybe that would be a good thing in this case. Maybe he could think of another way to do this that wouldn't require a bolt.

"After all," he said to Old Gray, who merely flicked

an ear at him and continued to graze nearby, "cavemen invented the wheel. Cavemen. I'm smarter than any caveman. I can do this."

He knelt closer. If he had some sturdy wire, even baling wire would work if he doubled it, he could go in through this part, loop it around, bring it through here, and then if he had some kind of large metal nut, he could use that to brace the wheel on.

He had it. The bolt he'd gotten from St. Paul earlier in the spring came with a nut. He could use that. Where had he put it?

The logical place would be with all the extra parts he kept on hand, but he chuckled. Just because it was logical didn't mean it would be there.

He wandered back into his house and stood at the door.

"Metal nut, metal nut, where did I put you?" he mused softly.

In the parlor, he pawed through the contents of the desk. He found a picture of Olea when she was ten, but no nut.

In the kitchen, he upended the junk drawer and discovered, to his delight, the key to the grandfather clock. Maybe he could get the thing to work again now.

In his bedroom, he looked through the stuff that had accumulated on the top of his dresser. There were two church notices—one funeral and one wedding—two stamps, four coins, a marble, and a cardboard disk advertising the Grange. But no nut.

In the cellar, there was nothing on the shelf that ran

the perimeter except dust and little crunchy things he didn't want to think about.

Where else could it be?

The outhouse? No. He'd already checked the barn.

Jacey's room. He entered the boy's bedroom, smiling at the sheer boyness of the decor. He didn't want to snoop, but he did have to find that bolt.

He quickly examined the drawers of the bureau, moved the bureau itself out from the wall, and flopped to the floor to look under the bed. No nut.

In the little closet? Nothing.

He was defeated. He was just not going to find this nut. He started out of the room, and as he did, he noticed something a bit odd with the cow in the window. The sunlight glinted off its halo.

Its halo? The cow had a halo?

In three long strides, he was at the window, the toy cow in hand. Indeed, cow had a halo—a halo created by a metal nut.

The boy had such a soft spot for animals, he thought, missing him again so much that he thought his heart would literally explode, that he would even put a halo on a cow.

His son couldn't come home too soon.

He heard a wagon pull into the farmyard, and, tucking the vital nut into his pocket, he went to see who his visitor was.

"Lars Olsen!"

"It is, it is."

"What's up with you today, my friend?" Ben asked.

"I was just enjoying the weather and saw Old Gray

here, and the cultivator out, and thought you might need some help."

"I do!"

Ben explained the plan for repairing the wheel on the cultivator, and Lars nodded. "I think it's going to work."

They sat cross-legged by each other and began to work.

"Of course it's not going as smoothly as I pictured it," Ben said. "I thought I could do this, and this, and this, and this, and twist, retrace my steps, and I'd be done."

"Nothing ever goes as smoothly as we picture it," Lars agreed, and Ben thought he heard a layer of glumness in the man's voice.

"Things going all right for you, Lars?" he asked.

For a moment Lars didn't answer, and then he shrugged. "Things go."

Ben didn't want to pry, so he continued on with his work, holding the wheel shaft steady so Lars could muscle the axle back on.

At last Lars said, "You think about love?" Except, tellingly, it came out as "You tink about love?" and Ben knew that Lars was nervous discussing the subject.

Ben froze in place. "Of course I think about love," he said cautiously. "I love my son. I love my God. Even Olea, although she tests me over and over, more than a really good sister should. Why?"

"What about a woman?"

"I think Olea is a woman," Ben said.

"I mean like love forever. You were married." Lars kept his eyes averted. "That was love."

Ben knew he had to choose his next words carefully. He'd always kept Cecelia's memory fairly well-preserved, even though their marriage had been the worst sham ever.

"Lars, that was a youthful marriage." There, that was noncommittal, and in being noncommittal, spoke volumes if his friend was willing to listen.

"I'm not youthful."

"Nor am I."

"So is a union in your later years—do you think love is—can you think—what makes you think she loves you?"

Ben stared at him. "What a question, Lars!"

"Is a good question. Is love just for young sprouts, or can it catch you?"

Can it catch you? The image was startling. Had it caught him already? He had found himself thinking about Mariah a lot, but on the other hand, he was a farmer in Dakota. It wasn't like he had a lot of other things to occupy his mind. Sometimes he thought his brain must look like the prairie—open and wide, with nothing to dot the landscape.

Maybe he should take up philosophy. Perhaps try to teach himself Greek. He'd long ago decided to read the Bible straight through, even the *begat*s, but he hadn't gotten very far at all with that. He hadn't even made it out of Genesis.

That's what he'd do. Tonight he'd take his Bible out and read Genesis, and then Exodus, and then Leviticus, and Numbers. He realized with horror that he couldn't, at this moment, remember what came next.

Yes, this was going to be a worthwhile way to fill his mind and not let it become populated with Mariah—Mariah in the thistles, Mariah in church, Mariah in the wagon.

"I'm not in love with her," Ben said, his words a bit chilly.

Lars gaped at him but didn't respond. And then, after a moment, both men went back to work, laboring together under the summer sun; and with Lars providing the extra heft needed to make the wire twists hold, they eventually got it fixed.

"I think you're good to go there," Lars said, wiping his hands on the back of his overalls as he stood up.

"Thanks," Ben said as they walked back toward Lars's wagon. "I really appreciate the help. And Lars," he added as his friend heaved himself onto the wagon bench, "I'm really not in love with her. She's not sticking around here anyway."

Lars planted both hands on his knees and leaned forward, a grin so wide that it swallowed up the lower part of his face. "That's where you're wrong. That's where you're very wrong." He turned around and picked up the reins and clucked to his horse. "Time to go now."

He was actually laughing as he drove away. "Not sticking around indeed!" he called over his shoulder.

Ben went inside and got his Bible and opened it to Genesis 1. There was no time like the present to fill his mind with the Word.

Chapter 4

It was amazing how one day you could feel as if a dark cloud were looming over your head, and the next day it was all sunshine and daisies, Mariah thought as she sat in front of the little house.

She'd changed the curtains and re-covered a few pillows, and the house already felt warmer and more inviting.

It was a beautiful day, though, and it was not one to spend inside, no matter how lovely the curtains and pillows might be. Sunshine poured across the prairie, and insects buzzed and birds chirped, and from the farms in the area, cattle lowed and horses neighed and dogs barked.

The Dakota Territory had its charm, she had to give it that.

Would she find it as appealing, a quarrelsome little voice asked, if Ben weren't part of it? What if she were here by herself? Would she like it then?

Ben. She was an honest woman, and she had to confess that he was extremely handsome. What she especially liked was his quick smile in response to something she said, and his ready laughter.

But men were everywhere. Attractive men. Men who could smile and who could laugh and who could charm the skin off a snake. Right?

Mariah let her head drop back so the sun's warmth could wash over her face. It was so relaxing, she could almost fall asleep. So calm, so very calm, that she almost missed the response to her own query: Wrong question. The right question was: *Ben?* No more words than that. Just, *Ben?*

And the answer was *Maybe.*

She tried to imagine him charming the skin off a snake, but the sun was too comforting, and the air was so perfect, and she fell asleep.

The sound of a wagon approaching woke her up. It was Ben.

"Some of the men are gathering at the church to rehang a door. It won't take long, but it's that big door, and it'll take three or four of us to do it. So I volunteered, and I thought maybe you'd want to come along. Do you want to visit Prospect for a bit?"

What a brilliant suggestion! This couldn't have been better made for her.

"Sure," she said, trying to suppress the smile that rose to her lips. "I need some thread anyway."

If her good fortune held, she'd pick up some information along with her thread today. Meggin Sanders seemed like the kind of person who knew all sorts of interesting things. If anyone in Prospect knew about Joshua, it would probably be her.

Ben was oddly quiet on the ride in. Usually he kept a nice stream of conversation going, but today he seemed muted, almost reluctant to start any line of dialogue. Instead, he hummed under his breath. Hymns.

"You have a lovely voice, by the way," she said to him. "I noticed that in church, too."

"Thank you." A quick smile flickered across his face—surely she hadn't imagined that—before he returned to his personal hymn sing.

She saw, too, that he had his Bible with him. He caught her glance at it and said only, "I'm fulfilling a long-held promise to myself. I'm reading it straight through."

Something had shifted, something had changed, but she didn't know what it was, and she probably didn't want to hear the answer.

So she asked, conversationally, "It's a noble project. How far are you?"

"Genesis."

She turned before he could see her smile.

As they pulled into town, he suddenly asked her, "Have you noticed anything odd about Lars Olsen?"

"Odd? I barely know the man, and certainly not enough to know odd from normal with him. Why do you say that?"

He shook his head. "I wish I could explain. I don't

know. He's not paying attention to his crops this year. His fields are a mess, and I don't know what he'll get as a harvest. I don't know if I should say something to him, and if I did, what would I say, anyhow? 'Lars, you know you really have to plant your crops and weed them?' He's not two. He knows that."

"Maybe something else is occupying his mind," she said.

"Like what?"

"I don't know. Maybe he's wanted for a capital crime in Washington, DC! Or he's really a king of a far-off land who's lost his memory and is wandering the Midwest looking for it. Or he's truly the world's worst farmer and the other years have been sheer luck?"

He laughed. "Point taken. I don't know any more than you do. Ah, here we are at Meggin's."

He dropped her off at the store and went on to the church. She promised him that, yes, she'd come to the church when she was done, and that, no, it wasn't too far for her to walk, and, yes, she'd enjoy the stroll in the lovely weather.

She paused inside the door of Sanders Mercantile. Most men under the age of seventy were out on the land on a day like today, and they left the seats around the pickle barrel to their elders, those who had retired from farming or whatever job they had done in their younger years. A couple of male voices floated from the corner, two elderly gentlemen reminiscing about harvests past.

"Went five days without a lick of sleep," declared

one. "The corn was coming in that fast. This was down in I-o-way. I was near a dead one by the time I finally got it all in, and then I slept for forty-two hours straight."

"Yes, yes, indeed!" agreed the other one with a crackled laugh. "I recall those days. Too many times I fell asleep in the wagon, and once I even woke up in the barn, in the wagon with the reins in my hands, with Melchior the horse still attached. He was a good horse. Knew to bring us both home."

Another voice joined in, and she recognized it as Lars's. What was he doing here? Ben had said he was concerned about Lars's farming this year, that it had seemed lax, that he seemed to spend more time by the pickle barrel than in the fields. Was he all right? Was his health imperiled?

She was about to go check on him when Meggin's voice rang out. "Lars Olsen, please go to the cellar and bring up a case of Two Tulips tonic water. And put it under the counter at the end."

"Yes, ma'am." Lars stood up and lumbered away before Mariah could ask him how he was.

She turned to go to the notions counter, and as she did, her eyes fell upon a book about animals.

She picked up the small volume and leafed through it. Joshua would like this, she thought, especially the funny picture of the monkey hanging from a tree. She could almost see his face light up with enjoyment.

"That's a sweet little book," Meggin said at her elbow, startling Mariah. She hadn't realized Meggin had left her usual post at the counter.

"Yes, it is. I was thinking how much my nephew would like it." Her voice almost cracked on the words.

"You know, Ben's little guy's been hankering after it. Wait till you meet him. Just as bright as a button, he is."

Mariah put the book back down. If she had enough money later on, she'd buy it for Joshua. If she found him. If she could get him back. If she could—

"I'll take it." Mariah opened her purse and took out the coins.

The purchase left her nearly broke, but it reassured her. It was an act of faith, and the process left her with a calm sense of security that she would be reunited with her nephew.

"You want me to mail that for you?" Meggin's words intruded into her thoughts.

"What? Oh no, that's fine. I'll—I'll hang on to it until I see him."

Meggin's chubby face softened into a cherubic smile. "The little fellow's coming out here?"

Mariah shook her head. "No, well, yes. Actually, I'm not sure."

Meggin wrapped the book in a piece of brown paper. "There," she said, handing it to Mariah. "That'll keep it nice until you give it to him. I'll bet his mother's going to be right pleased, too."

"She's dead." Mariah's statement was barely audible.

"Oh my." Meggin's face crumpled with compassion. "I'm so sorry to hear that. Then the little angel's with his daddy."

"No. He's—he's gone, too."

Meggin's hands clasped in front of her ample bosom. "That's a tough row to hoe, losing both parents." She clucked sympathetically. "Has he got a good home?"

The words slipped out before Mariah could stop them. "He will—with me."

Meggin beamed. "That's wonderful. I know you'll be a top-notch mama to the tyke."

Suddenly Mariah felt as cagey as a master criminal. Here was the opening she needed to begin asking questions.

"I hope I can do him justice," she said, keeping her eyes downcast. "After all, I've never been a parent."

"Nobody is until the good Lord gives it to them," Meggin said heartily. "And being a good parent isn't something that comes with giving birth—it comes with giving love. It's from the heart, not the womb."

"You sound like you know what you're talking about." Mariah tried not to sound sly. "Are there others out here like me? You know, who are parents of a child not born to them?"

Meggin tsked. "It all becomes the same."

Drat it all. The woman was not coming across with any information. Mariah tried again. "But it would be nice to talk over my concerns with others in the same position."

"You need someone to talk to, you come to me. I've raised nine myself." Meggin gave Mariah an angled look. "Or better still, talk to Ben. He'll understand as well as anybody."

Good heavens. Was Meggin trying to push her into some sort of romantic alliance with Ben? Then Mariah realized that Meggin was only referring to the fact that both she and Ben were parenting without the benefit of a spouse.

"I suppose that's true," Mariah admitted. But she didn't tell the kindly woman that would never happen. As soon as she found Joshua, she'd leave the Dakota Territory.

With Joshua.

And Ben would have to struggle with parenthood on his own.

The thought brought a twinge to Mariah's chest, somewhere in the region of her heart. But she quickly squelched it with the thought of Joshua somewhere out here in the Dakota Territory feeling abandoned.

Ben would be all right by himself. He didn't need her. And she certainly didn't need him.

The Bible said that everything had a purpose. And hers was to get Joshua out of here. But she wouldn't be able to unless she had some money. And to have money, she had to sew these shirts.

Mariah tilted her chin up and smiled at Meggin. "I need some thread."

Ben stood just inside the post office and leafed through the mail. Rehanging the door hadn't taken as long as everyone had expected, and they were through early. He'd decided to stop at the post office on the off-chance there was a letter for him. He smiled in relief when he saw the pale-pink envelope with the curly handwriting.

It was from Bo's mother, and inside, folded very carefully, were four sheets of paper. The first was a drawing Jacey had made of a place near Lake Como in St. Paul. Bo's mother had written an explanatory line on the bottom of the page. He had apparently been quite taken by some plants called Victoria water platters, which grew in a lily pond, as he had drawn them over and over on the page.

The second was a scene of a big building. Outside it, on the walkway in front, were animals that looked like small horses. Maybe they were cats or dogs. One was halfway in the doorway of the building, and another was lying beside the sidewalk with his feet up in the air.

Ben chuckled at that because it looked so much like a grown-up might draw a dead animal, but with Jacey, it must be a cat taking a nap or something.

Above the building, in a cloud, was a man's face, with two big triangles sticking out of each side. In one window, a woman laid sideways, her eyes closed, and another woman was approaching the building with what looked like a big box dangling from her hand.

Sprinkled throughout the sky were what must have been snowflakes.

What an odd drawing, Ben thought, but he knew that the mind of a six-year old was wildly imaginative.

The third sheet was a note from Jacey himself. Bo's mother must have helped him with it, because many of the words had been written in her clear handwriting. But most of the note was in Jacey's own distinctive one-inch-tall letters. "Deer Dad," he read, "I am having good time. We have gon to the park and saw thes flowrs. I also drawd this for yu. I mis yu. Lov, Yr Son."

Bo's mother had written a message on the fourth page:

Jacey did these two drawings one night when he was having trouble sleeping. The one of the building needs a lot of explanation, and I will explain more when we get back. Briefly, it is of his life before he came here. The man in the sky is his father, the woman in the window is his mother, and the woman coming inside is his aunt. He told me her name, but I couldn't understand it. I didn't ask too much because he was starting to get upset. You may want to talk to him about this because those animals, Ben, are rats.

He rubbed his hand over his face and tried to stay composed.

Rats.

He wanted to go to St. Paul that very minute and get Jacey and hug away the bad memories, but he knew that no amount of love could make them vanish. But love could make them tolerable.

Mariah walked along the street, swinging her bag with the thread and the book in it. She hadn't gotten far with Meggin, but perhaps she had planted some seeds that might bear fruit later on.

She had to stay positive like that.

As she walked by the post office, she glanced inside. Ben stood by the bank of mailboxes, a pink envelope in his hand.

She tried to quell the sudden resentment that arose in her. So he got a letter in a pink envelope. Probably half of the world was female, and he had a sister and a mother and whatever relatives. Or it could be a friend.

Or a woman he was romantically involved with.

It was none of her business, absolutely none at all. She squared her shoulders, raised her chin up, and headed in.

He began talking to her all at once, but her eyes were caught by a flyer that was stuck to the wall. It was fly-spattered and torn around the edges, but it was still there, eight months later, for her. No one had taken it down.

ORPHANS AND FOUNDLINGS
Of New York City, New York
Bring you
"The Orphan Train"
Fargo, Dakota Territory
17 January 1887
Grange Hall
2:00 PM
Open your heart and save a child today
Children of all ages available
For adoption
Boys and girls

She couldn't breathe. She walked behind Ben, as if in a dream, and stared at the flyer.

It was real. With this broadside, she knew she was close to her nephew. She looked around her surreptitiously. No one was watching—Ben was studying the letter he held—and she quickly snatched down the announcement and folded it, sliding it into her bag.

"Mariah? Have you heard anything I've said?"

She turned to him and brought herself back to the here and now with a snap. "I'm sorry," she said. "I was totally in a fog for a minute."

"Well," Ben said, "I got a letter from my son, and some drawings. Do you want to see them?"

"Of course I do." She took them and leafed through them uncomprehendingly. Children's drawings all had a certain degree of sameness about them. Big heads, stick arms with gigantic stick fingers, and stick legs. These might even have been her nephew's drawings. He'd sent her similar ones.

She handed them back to Ben. "He's quite an artist. I can't wait for you to meet him," he said.

She didn't want to seem like a petulant child, but suddenly the fact that Meggin talked about Ben's child, and Ben talked about him, and how terrible it was for the little guy to be away from his father—it was too much. Her nephew was away from family forever.

Put on a scale, his situation far outweighed that of Ben's son.

On the way home, the situation that had gone on on the way to Prospect was reversed. Now Ben was chatty, talking about his son's return, while Mariah didn't want to speak. The flyer that was in her purse had first seemed like such a hopeful thing, but now it almost seemed as if it were taunting her: *You may never find him.*

"I'll pick you up for church tomorrow morning?" Ben asked as he pulled up in front of her small home, and she nodded, almost numbly.

Mariah got out of the wagon, more than a little out of sorts. The entire way back from Prospect, Ben had talked about his son coming home soon, and she tried not to let it bother her, but it did. She was glad for him, pleased beyond measure that his household would once again be intact, but it simply highlighted how incomplete hers was.

Joshua should be coming home—to her. That was the way it should be.

Mariah sat through the next day's church services, but very little of what the minister said had an impact. She'd barely slept the night before, tossing in her bed as she turned over the day's events. It was almost too much to take in.

But one part of the service did stay with her. The sermon had been about the promises of God to His people, she'd gotten that much. He'd used the last line of Genesis, chapter eight: "While the earth remaineth, seedtime and harvest, and cold and heat, and summer and winter, and day and night shall not cease."

She'd always loved that verse for the comfort it offered. Nothing would end. She clung to it again, repeating it over and over until it gave her the solace she needed.

The afternoon was glorious with sunshine, and she had just pulled a chair into the shade to have a cup of tea when Ben rode into the farmyard.

"Guess what I just got!" he announced. "A side of beef! I'm getting it tomorrow, and I'll bring over a slab of it for you."

"I can't take that," Mariah said, but he brushed her words away.

"Charles Conway gave me a side in exchange for my helping him rebuild his barn last month."

"I don't want to take it from you."

"Why shouldn't you?"

"How long did it take you to rebuild that barn?"

"A week, maybe two, all told. Why?"

"Well, for heaven's sake, Ben! You need it to feed your son when he gets back. You should preserve it for that. Plus it'd be like taking a week's wages from you!" she exclaimed.

Ben roared with laughter. "This is only a bit of a side, not the whole thing." He cocked an eyebrow at her. "Say, have you ever seen a cow or a steer?"

"Of course I have!"

"Really?"

"We certainly had books in Massachusetts, Ben Harris. Just because this is the end of zero doesn't mean the rest of the world is ignorant." She tried to look dignified. "I've seen cows."

"A picture of a cow, or a real live, in-the-flesh beast?"

"Um, a picture." Her eyes flashed defiantly. "But it was a good picture."

"Okay." He grinned, clearly amused by the turn this conversation was taking.

For heaven's sake, what did he find so funny? What was going on with him?

"How big is a cow, Mariah? Want to tell me?" He casually examined a scratch on the back of his hand. Mariah had the uncomfortable feeling he was trying hard not to laugh at her.

"Ummm, big." She nodded. "Pretty big." His grin grew. "Really big." He was smiling openly. "Really, really big."

"If you wanted to put your hand on a cow, where would you put it?" he asked.

"I beg your pardon? Why on earth would I want to touch a cow?"

"If you wanted to reach out and put your hand on a cow, well, just show me how you'd be standing. Where would your hand rest?"

"Would I be putting it on the cow's, um…" She bit her lip. She couldn't say it. It seemed, well, immodest somehow.

He looked at her, his head tilted to the side as he awaited the rest of her question.

She took a deep breath and said it. "Would I be putting my hand on the cow's waist?"

Ben lost his effort to contain his mirth. He doubled over as rolls of laughter overtook him. He chortled. He guffawed. He hooted.

Blood raced into Mariah's face. Her first thought had been right. She shouldn't have said it.

She dropped her head and studied him surreptitiously from under a golden fringe of eyelashes and hair. Suddenly she realized with amazement that he didn't think that what she had said was improper. No, he was laughing at her!

But why?

"A cow—a cow—a cow's waist!" he choked out at last.

"I don't see what's so funny," Mariah said, straightening her back and trying to look stately.

"A cow's waist!"

Finally, with difficulty, he stood.

He leaned over and squeezed her arm, still wiping the tears of laughter from his eyes. "Mariah, a cow is one big creature. You don't have to worry about this meat I'm giving you. It's just a tiny bit of the whole animal. If you wanted to put your hand on its waist"—he was clearly trying to contain the laughter that bubbled up at the word—"Oh, Mariah, sometime you've just got to meet a living, breathing steer face-to-face. And please, let me be there to see it!"

He left the house, still laughing. "A cow's waist! A cow's waist!"

The next day Ben chuckled again at Mariah's understanding—or lack of it—about a cow's anatomy as he prepared the beef to take to her. She was truly a precious one.

He wrapped the meat carefully—it wouldn't do to

have it spoil in the afternoon's warmth—and laid it on the floor of the wagon, out of the sun's rays. He had some other errands for the day, including changing the hay in the stable at Mariah's home. He'd brought Karl and Lainie's animals to his house when they left, but the hay still needed to be turned and aerated.

When he arrived, she was outside, studying the front of the house. She paced from one side to the other, scratching out occasional marks in the dirt with a long stick she carried.

"What are you doing?" he asked as he laid the reins down and jumped out of the wagon. "Go on, old man," he said to the horse as he unhooked it. The horse wouldn't go far.

"I'm planning something. What would you think about a lilac bush here"—she pointed with the stick to a spot by one side of the door—"and here?" She indicated a similar spot on the other side of the door.

"Lilacs? Here?"

He looked around him. The house had fallen into great disrepair since Lainie had come into the family way and needed so much help. Of all the places to start, planting a lilac tree was not where he would have begun.

The door that hung on one hinge. The window sills that were cracked. The front steps that were nothing more than two chunks of building stone that Karl had gotten as leftovers from a building project in Fargo.

The roof leaked. The chimney—oh, he'd forgotten about that. He'd better see to that before winter set in, or the house would be aflame the first time she used it, there were so many gaps in the flue.

He should have done those things earlier, but there had been so much going on that he'd let the repairs drop. He silently vowed to take care of those soon, even if it meant working literally from sunup to sundown.

"Here's the meat," he said. "I need to see to the hay."

She took the packet and thanked him, and then disappeared inside the house. When she came out, she ran to the stable and caught up with him just as he was entering it.

"Can you tell me," she said, "why you do this with the hay since there aren't animals here? I have thought about it, and for the life of me, I can't determine a good reason."

"Come with me," he said, taking the pitchfork from the wall.

They approached the first corral, and she wrinkled her nose.

"You're starting to get the idea," he said.

With one quick jab of the pitchfork and a toss of the hay that lay across the floor, the pungent smell arose and enveloped them.

Sometimes a single breath was worth a thousand words. It smelled horrendous, and she recoiled.

"It'll mildew because, even though it's dry, it does have some moisture content, and I wouldn't be surprised to learn that some rain gets in here, too. You let this stuff mildew, and you'll have critters in here that will take this building down."

"Mice," she said, her hand over her nose.

"More than that. Rats and skunks and bugs, and at least a snake or two. Where you have rats and mice, you'll have snakes. The food chain, you know."

"Oh, well that's just wonderful. Rats and mice and snakes." She shuddered. "And people raise children here!"

"But possibly worse than that is—"

She interrupted him. "Worse? What could be worse?"

"Fire."

"How can there be a fire if the stuff is wet?"

"Put your hand in there now, Mariah."

"No, thank you, I don't believe I'll do that," she said, stepping back and tucking her hands behind her back like a little girl.

"Will you believe me, then, when I say that the warm, moist hay generates heat, and somehow that I can't begin to explain to you, it combusts, and the next thing you know, the barn is on fire, and then the house, and then the fields."

She raised her hands in front of her in defeat. "All right. Have at the hay. I'll be outside where it smells much better, or it will when I get my lilacs in."

As he pitched the old hay out of the barn, he thought of her choice of words. *My lilacs.*

Perhaps that meant she would stay? A crazy new hope blazed through his veins.

He remembered how Lars had said she was going to stay. But how did Lars know?

He shook his head. There was much in this world he did not understand.

He finished tossing out the old hay and leaned on the pitchfork to catch his breath. He'd heard rumors—nothing more than that, just rumors—that Karl and Lainie weren't coming back and were planning to abandon the claim and the house. It made everything easier—and more complicated.

If they came back, Mariah would have to find another place to live, or she'd need to move away.

If they didn't come back, Mariah could stay there for as long as she wanted. The claim papers wouldn't be a problem. He was already in line for this claim if Karl let it go.

It all circled back to Mariah, and what she wanted to do.

If she only had something to keep her here, something that was the anchor she seemed to need. Whatever drove her out to Dakota would have to be resolved. But equally important was that something would have to be put in its place.

Like Jacey. The boy had given him life in ways he'd never expected. He made each day a new experience filled with joy and surprise.

Jacey! He'd be back soon!

He could barely wait to introduce him to Mariah. He was such a good boy.

And by the time he got here, who knew? Ben might be well into Leviticus.

Ben put the pitchfork back on the wall of the barn. He wouldn't replace the hay today. There wasn't really much point. The only animal that ever ate it was his own horse Old Gray on his trips over. It was just as easy to bring some in the back of the wagon, and throwing a bale onto the ground was certainly easier than the back-breaking task of grubbing out a corral.

He wiped his face and stepped back into the sunshine, blinking his eyes after the darkness of the barn.

Mariah was still there, pacing out the area in front of the door. Now, though, she was drawing large circles in the dirt and frowning.

"Still figuring out the lilac situation?" he asked, mopping the back of his neck with his handkerchief.

"I am. It seems to me that the bushes I saw in Fargo were at least ten feet across, and probably twelve feet along. Height, I'm guessing seven, maybe eight feet tall?"

He grinned. "You planning to leave any room for the house? Those things would dwarf it!"

"True," she admitted with a laugh. "Maybe a bit smaller would be a good idea."

"Each plant is its own size," Ben said, "and it depends on the kind of lilac, the age of it, and the sunlight and water, too, I'd imagine."

"I understand that. Well, I'm going to need a ride into Fargo to get me two lilacs."

"And who do you think is going to give you this ride?" he asked.

"You?" she said, tilting her head to the side.

He shook his head. "No, Mariah. I'm not travelling all the way to Fargo on a wild goose chase to get a couple of lilac bushes."

"Can I get them in Prospect?"

"No. Unless you find some growing wild down by the river, but I doubt it."

"So I'll go to Fargo."

"Harvest is nearly upon us, and you want me to take a day off and go to Fargo with you?"

"Can I borrow the wagon and Old Gray?" she countered. "You really don't need to come along, too."

"Where would you get them in Fargo?" he asked.

"I'll find out before I leave. I'm not a know-nothing," Her eyes were starting to flare with anger.

"The fact is, Mariah, that even if you do plant the lilacs, do you know how to do it? Do you know anything at all about lilacs? Anything? Have you ever planted even a radish? Remember the thistles you got in your fingers when you first arrived? And what will you do if, after all this work, the plants don't thrive? This dirt beside the house is just clay and sand basically. This is the only spot in the whole valley that doesn't have good soil. No. This is a fool's errand, and while it may make all the sense in the world to you, it doesn't to me."

Mariah's face flared red as blood shot up her neck to flood her cheeks. Abruptly she stood, bristling like an annoyed hen.

She pulled her skirts around her and marched back into the house, her hair blazing around her head in a golden-red halo.

Ben stared after her. What could he have done that set her off so? He ran the conversation in his head again, and he groaned as he realized what he'd said, and how she'd interpreted it. *Fool's errand.* What had he been thinking?

"Mariah!" he called as he leaped to his feet. "Mariah, you've got it all wrong! I didn't mean it that way!"

Her head stuck around the edge of the blanket screen she'd disappeared behind. "Well, if you didn't mean it, then why did you think it?" She glared at him and popped back behind the curtain.

Ben stopped midstride. "If I didn't mean it, why did I say it? If I didn't think it, why did I mean it? What on earth did you say?"

"I said, 'If you didn't say it, then why did you think it?' " Mariah yelled from her hiding place. She paused, and started again. "No, I mean, if you didn't mean what you tried to say…"

She threw open the curtain and stomped outside. "Oh, I don't know what I said. I don't even know what I meant. Or what I meant to say. Or thought to say."

Ben looked at her. She was disgruntled, rubbing her forehead. Her face was worked into a deep frown.

He couldn't help it. He burst out laughing, and she joined him, and soon she and Ben were sitting beside each other on the floor as wave after wave of laughter rolled out of them.

He hadn't laughed this hard in months, and it felt so good, so cleansing, he didn't want to stop.

When the laughter subsided to chuckles, Mariah wiped her eyes.

"Well, whatever I said, I'm sure I meant it," she said at last.

"And I'll do my best to do whatever it is," he solemnly agreed. "Or not to do what it isn't." He scratched his chin. "Or to do what it isn't, or—"

"Unless you think that you mean that it isn't what you said because you thought it was the thing that wasn't it after all." She beamed at him.

A fresh wave of laughter threatened his newly re-gained composure.

"Stop it, stop it, stop it!" Mariah said, gasping as she caught her breath.

He stood and grinned. "All right. I've got to go take care of Old Gray, anyway."

But he didn't leave right away. Mariah's eyes sparkled like clover in the sun and then mellowed.

The words came out of her mouth in one long stream. "Thank you for laughing with me, Ben. It's—it's been a long time since I've laughed like this."

"You have a nice laugh, Mariah Rose," he said at last, lifting her chin with his fingertips. "It's like the soft chiming of bells. I'd like to hear it more often."

It had felt so cathartic, so refreshing to laugh at last, that he hated to go.

She sat on the front step, between the place where the two lilacs would go, and he slewed around in his seat and watched her as he rode off toward his house, her shape and the outline of the tiny house becoming smaller and smaller on the horizon until at last both disappeared where the land met the sky.

"You know what would make this place more like a home?" Mariah asked Olea. They were in the little house, trying to process some of the vegetables that were threatening to overtake the kitchen.

"A baby crying, three children fighting over an apple, the dog howling because its tail is stuck in the oven door, and a pile of dirty clothes that are so desperate for attention that they nearly walk over to you and leap into the tub on their own?"

The two women were spending the day together, putting up jars of early tomatoes and green beans. With three gardens—Mariah's, which produced on its own with no help from her, and Ben's, which was neat and orderly and productive, and Olea's, which was a combination of the two—they were struggling to keep up with the produce.

Mariah laughed. "That would do it!"

"Did you have brothers and sisters?" Olea's attention was on the stack of beans she was cleaning, and she didn't notice the sudden stiffening of Mariah's back.

She did not want to talk about Lorna. Not yet, anyway. Not until she'd fulfilled her promise to herself to find Joshua and get him back to civilization, back to New York or Massachusetts.

Instead she answered, "It certainly wasn't as bad as that! No, what would make this place a home would be a lilac bush." She began filling the kitchen with words, hoping to redirect the conversation back to where it had begun. "They were in bloom when I arrived. There was a beautiful big one in Fargo, just down the street from the hotel where I stayed. The flowers were a gorgeous shade of lavender, and it smelled absolutely heavenly. I told Ben I want to plant some by the front door."

"Lilacs are good here. They winter really well, which is surprising since the—" Olea looked up, and the knife stopped midslice. "Are you saying what I think you're saying? That you're going to stay here? In this house?"

She put the knife down, wiped her hands, and hurried around the table to wrap Mariah in a great bean-scented hug. She released her and then hugged her again. "Oh, that's wonderful news! Karl and Lainie were nice enough, but it would be better to have you here. I'm so glad you're going to stay! I said to Fred just last night that I thought you were softening about staying here, and maybe—"

"No! Wait! What?"

"You said you wanted a lilac bush so you could make this your home." Olea stared at her as if she'd lost her senses. "You remember. You said it not even one minute ago."

"I said a lilac bush would make this *a* home, not that it would make it *my* home. That's a huge distinction, Olea."

"But I thought you were happy here."

The statement caught her off guard. Happy? What was happy? She hadn't been happy for—she drew a blank. She had no idea when the last time was that she'd been really happy, not for any length of time. Oh, there were moments here and there, scattered throughout her life, when she had been cheerful or glad and, yes, maybe briefly, not sad.

All of her efforts had gone initially to working, and then to this trip. She must never forget that her goal on this trip was to find Joshua and bring him home.

Then she could be happy.

Something little and annoying tickled her heart with a barrage of questions: *Could you, really? Honestly? Would that make you happy? Finally?*

She pushed the irritating voice down, holding it until it was silenced, and sewed a fake smile onto her face.

"I'm happy. Always was, always will be."

Olea studied her. "Have you ever been in love, Mariah?"

The smile started to crack. "What an odd inquiry," she answered stiffly.

Olea put her hand on Mariah's arm. "It's not odd, I think, not between friends, and we are friends, aren't we?" she asked softly.

Wonderful, Mariah thought. There was another part of her life she tried to ignore. She'd been so fixated on raising enough money to get Lorna and Joshua that she'd let her friends go. When she'd refused social engagements enough times, explaining that she was working extra hours at the mill or in the sample shop, they'd eventually drifted away from her.

And never much of a churchgoer from the start, she'd let that drop entirely, choosing instead to spend the hours catching up on badly needed sleep. Most Sundays she slept until noon or later, she was so exhausted.

It had all been worth it. All of it. She'd do it again in a heartbeat.

However, standing there next to Olea, her round, kind face so concerned, she realized how much she'd missed friendship.

"I have something to do," she said quietly, rising to get a new container of salt out of the cabinet and keeping her back to Olea so she wouldn't see the redness in her eyes, "and when I am done with that, I will have to leave."

"That sounds mysterious," Olea said. "And I hope you find whatever it is that makes you happy. Whoever it is that makes you happy."

The kindness in Olea's voice broke through the barrier, and Mariah put her hands over her face. Without turning around, she said, "My nephew is missing. I think he's somewhere in this area, but I don't know."

"Oh, dearie!" Olea leaped from her chair and flew to Mariah's side. "That must be the most horrible thing ever! What happened? What can I do?"

Mariah turned and buried her face in Olea's shoulder and sobbed. "My sister died, and some people took her son and brought him out here"—she waved her hand in a big circle without lifting her head—"and that's all I know. I'm not even sure he's here. As far as I know, he could be in Tennessee or Texas or Wisconsin. I don't know for sure, but in my heart, I think he's here."

"There, there," Olea soothed. "Come over here, and let's talk about this. Your nephew was kidnapped?"

"No," Mariah said, sniffing as she sat down. "Not exactly. You know those orphan trains?"

Olea nodded. "I do."

"I heard that Joshua was put on one of those. The organization in New York City wouldn't tell me anything, but I—I don't know how to explain it, but I am positive he's here, in the territory."

"What organization is that?" Olea asked, speaking slowly.

"Orphans and Foundlings. Wait." Mariah rose and got the announcement she'd taken from the post office and brought it back to Olea. "This is the group. Orphans and Foundlings."

"Have you talked to Ben about this?" Olea's gaze never left Mariah's face.

"No."

"Why not?"

"Because the man at the office of Orphans and Foundlings was so dreadful to me. He wouldn't tell me where Joshua was, just that he has a good home, and—"

"Let me interrupt you for a moment. Let's assume that he does have a good home. What would you do then?"

"His good home is with me," Mariah said, clenching her fist. "I want him to come back with me to Massachusetts and live a normal life, just the two of us, happily ever after."

"But it might be that he's been living with another family for, what, almost seven months now, and he might be settled in and happy."

Mariah shook her head. "No, and it's precisely this reasoning that made me decide not to tell anyone why I was here, but honestly, I'm not getting anywhere. I don't know who to ask. I don't know who to confide in. I probably shouldn't have confided in you."

Olea reached across the table and rubbed Mariah's hand. "No, your secret is safe with me. I'm not sure it's something that should be secret, though. Mariah, I really would like to pray with you over this. Would you be all right with that?"

Mariah nodded.

Olea began softly, "Dearest Lord, we're here, just the two of us and You, and we need some healing on Mariah's heart. You know her burden. She wakes with it, she carries it during the day, and at night it lays down in her soul. Please, dearest God, give her some respite. Show her the way she needs to proceed, and give her the strength to accept the outcome. Mariah, do you want to add anything?"

"You've shown me amazing things since I've arrived here, Lord," Mariah whispered, "and I appreciate it all, but I want to go home. I want to go home with my nephew. Please, let me go home." She tried to swallow down the fresh batch of tears. "Amen."

She raised her head and saw Olea's eyes brimming. "I understand," Olea said. "I do understand."

"There's something you have to square up," Olea continued. "I don't know what it's about or who it's with. You may at some point want to tell me. If you do, I'll listen. If you want me to remember, I'll remember. If you want me to forget, I'll forget. The only limitation is that I will not keep a secret from my husband. I will not promise not to tell him. He's a good man, though, Fred is, and if I ask him to keep it in his heart and not on his lips, he'll do it." She smiled. "He's well-trained."

Mariah swallowed and spoke. "Thank you, and I do appreciate it. But it's not something I can share at this time."

"I understand. I am here. I'm not going anywhere, and I'll always be available if you need a sounding post. I'm your friend."

"Thank you." The words came out as a whisper.

"We're all on your side." Olea patted her arm. "If you need someone to talk to, I'm here. Or Ben. And Fred—well, he'd listen, but he'll just look panicked. He's not used to having women talk to him."

Mariah laughed, the sound edging past the lump in her throat. "Fred is a good man."

"He is, indeed. I am quite blessed." She stood and returned to the worktable. "Blessed with more beans than a woman should have, that's for sure. I think I'll be slicing them in my sleep."

"I know what you mean." Mariah was grateful for the easy way Olea changed the subject. "And tomatoes, too. The best part, though, is that the smell is absolutely glorious, isn't it?"

"I'll dab some on behind my ears tonight and see if Fred notices."

Mariah began to blanch the tomatoes, dropping each ruby orb into the boiling water and pulling them out again quickly. The skin slid off easily then, making canning them much easier.

"You know," Olea said, sighing as she clipped the ends off the green beans, "the more I do this, the longer each piece gets. When I started, I was so careful. Each bean got snipped into one-inch pieces. Now, I don't even care if I cut them at all."

"And why should you? Ouch." Mariah pulled her hand back as the steam burned it. "It's nice having the beans cut into bite-sized pieces, but it's not like Fred can't cut his own vegetables."

"True. Well, that'll make things a lot easier here." With a quick sweep of her hand, Olea gathered the beans and dumped them in the jars. "The nasty ends are cut off. That's all they need."

"I don't know about you," Mariah said, "but as soon as these tomatoes are peeled, I'm going to take a break. This kitchen is getting quite hot, and I'm about as red as these things are!" She held a handful of bright-red tomatoes against her cheeks. "See?"

"Let's go outside now before I perish in here. Fred will come looking for me and find me here, a shadow of my former self, sprawled across the table, beans in my hair, and in a puddle of perspiration."

After rinsing off their hands and splashing their faces with the water in the basin—which had grown quite tepid—they went to the front of the house and sank onto the cracked wooden chairs that Mariah had put there to mark where the lilacs would be. Mariah's stake-backed seat creaked ominously, and Olea chuckled.

"We'd better get Ben or Fred over here to look at

that. I certainly don't want to plop down in it and find myself with my toes over my nose, thank you, dear."

Mariah fanned herself vigorously with her apron and shook her head. "I can do it. I like to sit out here and sew, so it's something I need to get moving on. Just as soon as I recover here and don't feel like I'm going to explode from the heat, I'll take a look at it myself."

"You'll fix it?" Olea grinned. "Since when have you gone into the furniture repair business?"

"I know as much as Ben or Fred, I suspect. How hard can it be? It's a piece of wood, and it's stuck to another piece of wood. If the wood's still in good shape, I'll hammer in a new nail. If the wood's not in good shape, then I have some firewood."

"I know you don't want to hear this, my friend," Olea said, "but you're turning into quite the frontier woman."

Lately Lars was spending more time near the pickle barrel than usual, and it seemed to Ben that Meggin was quick to ask the farmer to pick up a heavy box or get something off a shelf for her.

The last time he'd been at the mercantile, Meggin had asked him to bring out a crate of Lady Andrews's Magical Hair Restoration products from the storage area, and Lars was red and perspiring heavily by the time he had set it on the floor near the personal care products, and he'd looked so uncomfortable that Ben had feared that the man's heart might give out.

He'd stood, offering his help, but Lars had waved

him away. Too proud, Ben figured, to admit that he was being run ragged by a woman.

Meggin was, like Lars, of an indeterminate age. Built just like Lars, but always swathed in a spotless apron, she managed her store, every single inch of it. Her skin was permanently leathered from the sun, and she never stopped moving, wiping down the counters and sweeping the wooden plank floor. Olea had told him that a grain of dirt had no chance in that store, that a doctor could open a surgery and remove a person's spleen with complete confidence on Meggin's counters, they were so spotless.

Lars was a good farmer, but lately he'd been a bit lax about keeping up with the work. Ben had noticed that his seeds had gone in a week later than everyone else's, and the task had taken him a week longer, and the crop rows in his fields weren't as straight as they should be, although when he mentioned it to Olea and Fred when they were gathered together for dinner, they'd dismissed his concerns.

"I'm sure he's fine," Olea said with a laugh.

Fred nodded in agreement. "What's a week here or there? The harvest comes in."

"And a row doesn't need to be pencil-straight. Who said it did?" Olea added.

"Well, you want the rows to be linear," he began to explain, "because it makes the harvesting much easier, and the faster you can bring in the wheat, the better your chances are of making a profit and—" He stopped. Both Olea and Fred had smiles on their faces, and he knew they were teasing him.

"What?" he asked. "What? What am I missing here?"

Olea just shook her head. "Baby brother, you're missing nothing. Nothing at all."

He glanced at Fred in confusion. "Something just happened that I didn't catch at all," he said, hoping his brother-in-law would fill him in. "Want to let me in on it?"

Fred clapped him on the back. "Ben, there are some things that a fellow just knows, and some things a fellow has to learn."

He knew he was gaping at Fred, but he'd never heard the man be quite that cryptic in his entire life.

Fred grinned at him and raised one eyebrow, and Ben understood that all that was going to be said had been said…at least at the moment.

Still, he had to know.

"Here's my reason for asking," he said. "I'm not just a gossip. He was at my house not too long ago, helping me with the cultivator, and he began asking me all sorts of questions about who I loved, and didn't I think I was too old to fall in love. That kind of balderdash."

"Balderdash," Olea repeated softly.

"Seems like there's going to be a great crop of balderdash coming in this fall," Fred said, and he and Olea laughed.

"What did he ask you?" Olea grinned impishly. "And who was it about?"

"He wanted to know about being in love, and then I said something about well, she wasn't going to stick around, and—"

"Who isn't going to stick around?" Fred asked.

Ben turned away, but not before his sister saw the telltale flush. "Aha! I think my little brother is in love! I do!"

"I hardly know her," Ben muttered.

"And Adam hardly knew Eve. Boaz hardly knew Ruth. So if Ben hardly knows Mariah, does that mean he can't fall in love with her?"

Sometimes having a sister was the worst curse possible, Ben told himself. She never let up on him, never. She hadn't when they were little, and she sure wasn't changing her ways now.

He held up his hand. "I really do not want to discuss who I love—"

"See?" Olea said to Fred. "I was right."

"Or don't love, if you'd let me finish, but the point I am trying to make is that he said she's decided to stay."

"Who's decided to stay?" Fred asked with a wink.

"Let me ask this plainly. Is Mariah planning to stay?"

"Let me answer this plainly," Olea answered back. "Maybe but she doesn't know it."

"Oh, that clarifies it," he declared.

"Listen to me, Ben. Mariah has something that she needs to talk to you about. I know what it is, but I can't tell you because I made a promise not to. But I don't think telling you that is breaking the promise, is it?" Olea's brow wrinkled.

"Probably not," he said as reassuringly as he could, when what he really wanted to do was force her tell him what it was. When they'd been children, a quick threat of a worm in her bed or a toad in her lunch box was sufficient.

"Anyway, be prepared. And I wouldn't worry about what Lars said. It will all turn out in the end, I'm sure. You've brought her to church once. Bring her again," Olea said, and Fred nodded enthusiastically. "The day after tomorrow is Sunday, and we can all come over here after services and have a nice dinner."

"I think that sounds like a good idea," he said thoughtfully.

"Of course it's a good idea. I thought of it," Olea said. "Plus we, none of us, succeed on our own."

It was a good point, one worth thinking about.

Chapter 5

Once again, the church service spoke to what Mariah needed to hear. The text was Jeremiah 23: 23–25, "Am I a God at hand, saith the Lord, and not a God afar off? Can any hide himself in secret places that I shall not see him? saith the Lord. Do not I fill heaven and earth? saith the Lord. I have heard what the prophets said, that prophesy lies in my name, saying, I have dreamed, I have dreamed."

It brought Mariah back to the prayer that she and Olea had spoken together at the kitchen table. Her stomach ached as she tried not to think of what she had done to send her on this trip.

Certainly it was to get Joshua, but an equal part of it was to assuage her own guilty conscience. That bothered her. Why would that be paramount? Why did that eat at her worse than Joshua's disappearance?

She shut out the thoughts and returned to the service. They were standing to sing, and Ben held the hymnal for her, too.

He was so kind, this man. He would be good to love, to have as her helpmeet. She could see that, but first she had to get over some rather insurmountable hurdles.

First, she had to find Joshua.

Second, she had to forgive Ben for having a son. Usually it didn't bother her, but lately, as the date of his arrival neared, it became more of an issue.

Third, she had to accept the Dakota Territory. It was one and the same with Ben, and both were softening her heart, but once she found Joshua, she owed it to him to take him back East, where schools like Harvard and Yale were, ones that would make this boy the best lawyer or doctor possible.

Fourth, she had to find a way to forgive herself. That might never be possible.

The service was over, and she was no more settled for having been there. Her stomach twisted.

Olea and Fred spoke to them and reminded them that they were having dinner at their house.

"And," Fred said with a wink to Ben, "our barn cat has had kittens, and I think you might want to lay claim to one or two for the young man."

That did make her smile. Kittens were always a blessing. She'd take one, even, since she'd seen a mouse dropping in the kitchen.

No. No kittens. She wasn't staying, she reminded herself.

The ride to Olea and Fred's was too quiet, so she asked Ben how he was doing on his Bible project.

"I'm all the way to Exodus," he claimed proudly. "And I'm reading every single word, even when I don't exactly know what each word means."

"Good for you!" she said. "I think eventually it all makes sense. At least that's my hope."

The dinner was delicious at Olea and Fred's, but the best part was going into the barn and looking at the kittens. They were tucked in a far corner of a stall, on a soft stack of new hay, which Olea explained Fred had made as soon as he saw the kittens.

The mother, black with a white stomach, was proud of her babies, and let each one of the people hold the kittens.

"I don't know which one I like the most. The gray-striped one, or the black one with the white star on its forehead, or the fluffy one, or the gray and white one," Mariah said with a contented sigh. "I hate to think that I'd judge any of God's creatures, human or feline, on the basis of their skin color or fur color, but this gray and white one is a little doll."

"Are you keeping any of them?" Ben asked.

Both Olea and Fred shook their heads vehemently. "No, you can have any and all."

"What do you think?" Ben asked Mariah softly as the fluffy kitten tightened its miniature paws around his finger as it slept.

"I suspect you should let Jacey choose. And if he

doesn't choose the one you select, then I guess you have two cats."

"I suppose. And it's also—"

A sound at the barn door interrupted her.

"Hey! It's me! I wanna see! Let me have the kittens."

A small cannonball blasted through the barn door, past the adults, and zoomed right in on the kittens. "Oh, I want the gray stripey one! The fluffy one! Oh, the black one. And the one with gray and white spotches. I want them all! Can I have them all, Dad? Please!"

"Jacey," Ben said, "inside voices."

"But I'm not inside! Oh, by the way!" he shouted. "I'm home! Do you see me? I am home!"

"Okay, kitten voices. Use your kitten voice. Don't talk louder than the kittens. Sssh and listen. Do you hear how faintly they mew? No louder than that."

"Okay," the boy whispered loudly. "But I just wanted you to know I'm home."

"I think we already figured that one out, son. Give me a hug, and then there's someone else I want you to meet. Her name is Mariah."

The little boy wriggled free of his father's hug, and he looked at Mariah, his head tilted to the side.

"I know you," he said softly.

She nodded. After all this time, she couldn't speak, only nod.

"Auntie Mariah?"

She held out her hands to him, and he came to her in a willing embrace. He felt wonderful in her arms, all boyish muscle and skin and bone, and she didn't want to let him go.

"You know each other?" Ben asked.

"This is the reason I'm out here. The only reason." She smoothed back a stray lock of hair from Joshua's forehead. "I came to get Joshua."

"His name is Jacey." Ben knelt on the floor of the barn, behind the cats, frozen, as if unable to move.

"No, it's Joshua. Joshua Carleton Brighton. He's five years old."

"He's six," Ben said.

She only partially heard him. She couldn't stop looking at the boy and feasting her eyes on his round face and his eyes, so much like his mother's.

"How long have you been here?" she asked him.

"I don't remember. Dad?" Joshua turned around and looked at Ben.

Ben came and knelt beside Mariah and the boy. "Since January 17. It was a snowy day, remember?"

Joshua nodded. "And…" He looked down and then spoke so softly that Mariah had to strain to hear him. "And I might have told a little lie. Two lies. Well, one lie and one sort-of-not-a-lie."

Mariah couldn't stop smiling. He was here! She touched his face. "What were the lies?"

"I said I was six, and I wasn't. And the not-really-a-lie was that my name was Jacey. It came from Joshua Carleton. Get it? J. C. My friend on the train, Zena, gave me that name."

Mariah hugged him again. "You don't need to use the orphan train name anymore."

He pulled away. "But it's my name."

She nodded. "We'll talk about it later."

"I'm so glad you're here now, too," he said to her. "You're going to live with us, right?"

Both Ben and Mariah spoke at the same time. "Oh, no, no, no. No. No. No."

Joshua frowned. "Then how—?"

"Don't worry about it," Mariah said. "In a few days I'll take you back to Massachusetts, and we'll be happy again."

Joshua shook his head. "But what about Dad? Is he going with us?"

Mariah met Ben's eyes. "I don't think he will, honey."

Ben rubbed Joshua's back. "We all have a lot of talking to do, but I'm really glad that you found your Aunt Mariah. She loves you. We all love you, and we're glad to have you back with us."

He looked at Mariah over Joshua's head and mouthed to her, *We must talk.*

Their eyes locked, and for the first time since they'd met, the friendliness was veiled. Mariah knew that he wasn't going to give Joshua up easily, but it didn't really matter. She was his aunt, his blood relative, and she had the right to take him home.

"I have an idea," Ben said. "Why don't we all meet at our house for dinner, and afterward the adults will talk about, uh, things, when you're in bed."

"I don't want you to talk about things if I'm not there," Joshua said. "I have to be there. I do."

"Again, let's discuss this later. Meanwhile, why don't you tell us all about your trip?"

The boy regaled them with stories of his visit to St. Paul, Minnesota, most of them involving the legendary Bo and his apparently delicate stomach. They were tales of rolling down hills in the city—"It was so great because you know what happened? Bo threw up!"— and eating in fancy spots and from street carts—"And Bo threw up!"—and a trip on a steamboat—"And Bo threw up!"

Mariah couldn't quit looking at him. He looked a lot like his father, and only around his eyes could she see the resemblance to her sister.

It had been a long time since she had visited them. Her work schedule was relentless, but they wrote as often as they could, until at last the letters simply became fewer and fewer.

There was an amazing difference between a two-year-old and a five-year-old. There was so much they had to cover to make up for lost time.

Olea spoke up. "Why don't you take Jacey back to your house, Ben, and Fred and I will bring Mariah over in a while?"

"Joshua should stay with me!" Mariah protested, but Olea calmly motioned around her.

"You're not ready for him. Let him go back with Ben, and I'm sure we can work something out."

Mariah's heart nearly broke as she watched Joshua get into the wagon with Ben, but he was all smiles as they drove away, happily playing with the reins and waving at her.

"Come inside," Olea said, her voice inviting. "This is an amazing thing that has happened today!"

"It is!" Mariah said, her heart filled again with exultation. "I hope Ben understands why I need to take Joshua back with me though."

"Why 'Ben understands'?" Olea studied Mariah's face. "What about Jacey? Mariah, let's sit down."

The two women sank to the kitchen chairs. "I know that your heart is broken about your sister, and your nephew, too. I don't know what the answer is."

Mariah shook her head, not trusting her voice.

Olea's soft voice continued, "But at some point, you will have to decide what to do, and it has to be what's best for Jacey."

"For Joshua." Her throat contracted. "His name is Joshua."

"Joshua, then. He's so content here, Mariah. You saw him. You know what his face looks like when he sees Ben. It didn't take long, but those two have a bond."

Mariah didn't trust herself to speak. What she wanted to say was raging, hard, and awful.

"And he looks at you, and it's clear he loves you, too," Olea continued. "This is one of those difficult decisions. What are you going to do?"

"Why is it always what *I'm* going to do?" Mariah asked. "Why isn't it, *What is Ben going to do?* I've known Joshua since the second he was born."

Tears rose in her voice. "I was there, beside Lorna, standing in when her own husband couldn't. He didn't have the heart to see her in pain like that. But I was there. I held Joshua, wrapped him for her, handed him to her, touched his cheek as he lay across my sister's chest."

She fought for breath. "I watched him make his first sounds, saw him take his first steps, listened to him recite his alphabet. All of that. And you want me to give it up? Let some stranger have him? I was there, Olea. I was there, for his whole life!"

Olea whispered, "Not his whole life, Mariah. Not all of it."

The truth of what she said collapsed the world. When Joshua had needed her the most, when the time had come that more than anything else, she should have been there, she wasn't. And because of this, she'd lost him.

Her motivation had been good. Her intentions had been the best. Her love had been unswerving. But she'd failed him.

It was the one thing she hadn't been able to face, hadn't been able to confront even in her own mind. The only time the truth came to visit was on a sleepless night, when worry and fear took on monstrous sizes, way out of proportion to reality, and haunted those darkened hours with guilt.

Her soul was heavy with that guilt. It drove her onward, kept her from true happiness, insisted on chewing her heart until the pain was almost unbearable.

Yet even now, she couldn't confront it.

She had found Joshua, and now her heart was broken completely. The unfairness of it all was overwhelming. And perhaps, she thought, deserved.

* * *

Ben watched as Jacey slept. He had careened around the farmyard, hugging and kissing Old Gray and telling the horse he'd missed him so much his heart nearly broke. Old Gray simply stood patiently and waited for the torment to end.

Then Jacey had run into his room, touched each and every toy, punched his pillow, and run back outside, all the time singing, "I'm home and I'm home and I'm home and no more Bo throwing up."

Finally all of the excitement had been worked out of him, and he collapsed on his bed, fully clothed, one sweaty lock of hair drifting across his forehead.

Ben wanted to reach over and straighten his hair, but he was afraid of waking him up.

Oh, he was so afraid of everything now.

Mariah wanted to take Jacey from him. Legally, he didn't know what was the answer. As a relative, she probably had a greater claim on him, but on the other hand, the boy had been with him for months.

A soft knock on the door announced a visitor.

"Mariah! How did you get here?"

"I'd say I walked, but you'd know that wasn't true. I actually rode over here on a horse, one of Olea and Fred's. His name is Stonewall Jackson, and I think I know how he got it. The beast would tear down the road so I was clinging on for dear life, and then suddenly, it would just stop." Her hair was coming out of its bun, and she was working on sticking it back into place as she spoke.

"Are you okay? Did it throw you off?"

"I'm fine, although the horse might argue and say it's in pain. I kind of clung on to the mane when the reins whipped out of my hands at one point in the race. The nasty thing tried to snap at me with its big yellow teeth." She shuddered.

"So where is it now?"

"It might be outside, or it might be in another county, and I wish I could say I cared, but if I have to buy your sister and brother-in-law a new horse, everyone will thank me."

"I gather you didn't tie it up."

"Correct."

He peeked out the window and saw the horse silhouetted against the barn next to Old Gray. "I think Stonewall is telling my horse about the horrible escapade he just had to endure."

"They can have at it," she said with a flip of her hand.

"Can I get you some tea? Or coffee?"

She smiled. "Lemonade?"

"No, I don't have any."

"Tea is fine then."

Soon they were seated in the parlor, balancing china cups and sipping hot tea.

"I have to say, I didn't expect you to be this—" He struggled for the word.

"Pleasant?" she supplied. "Of course I'm pleasant. I have my son, and I am taking him home."

"Let's talk about the details, if you don't mind," he said. "You want to take him back to the East Coast, where you are his only living relative, if I understand you correctly."

"The way you say it makes it sound terrible," she objected. "There are plenty of children who thrive in a one-parent home."

"And this is also a one-parent home," he acknowledged, "but of course I also have Olea and Fred. Where would he live?" he persisted. "Do you have a house, perhaps with a yard or a park nearby, for him to get fresh air and exercise?"

"I don't have a house, no."

"An apartment?"

"Not at the moment. I gave it up to come out here."

"So you have no place to take him when you return."

"Oh, I'd find a home. Trust me on that."

"Certainly," Ben said, keeping his voice as level and quiet as he could, while staying alert for any sound of stirring from Jacey's room. "How would you return to the East Coast?"

"By train."

"Do you have the funds for tickets?"

"No," she said, her voice barely audible.

"I'm going to suggest something here, Mariah," he said. "Stay here a year. Build up your cash reserves, and make some plans."

"A year? Are you insane? I can't stay here a year. I can't last here a year."

"Why not?"

"Well, the culture. You have no opera, no drama, no—"

He grinned as he interrupted her. "And you attended all those things in Lowell?"

"No," she confessed. "I was too busy or too tired."

"I would invite you to discover Fargo and even Grand Forks further north. Those are cities on the move with cultural events, and they'll be much more accessible to you here."

"The weather is horrendous," she challenged. "You can't argue that with me."

"I'll give you that. We do have some extremely cold winters."

"And the schools. I want Jacey to have access to the best schools."

"He goes to school here."

"I want him to make the best use of his talents. Harvard would be an ideal spot."

He chuckled. "This about the boy whose recitation of his trip was punctuated by *and then Bo threw up.* I think we have a ways to go before signing him up for college. Plus we do have colleges here. The University of North Dakota in Grand Forks has been operating since 1883. It's new still, but we're mighty proud of it. It took on a lot of damage in the June tornado, but it's nothing a lot of Dakotan determination can't fix."

He took her hands in his. The gesture was comforting and reassuring. "I don't want to take your nephew from you. But I don't want to give him up—he is my son now. And above all, I don't think Jacey wants it to be an either/or situation. So here's my proposal: You stay for a year, look at the land, look at the people, and yes, even look at me. I'm very fond of you, and perhaps when this year is over, we can work on a completely acceptable plan."

"Wait. Are you asking me to marry you?"

He felt as if he were being pulled into a maelstrom. He had no choice but to abandon himself to the current. "I don't think so."

"Oh," she said flatly.

"Because in order for that to happen, I think I would have to kiss you first."

He couldn't believe he was saying these things.

And even more startling was how much he wanted to do just that.

"Let's do this," she said, pulling her hands free. "Let's put this lilac tree into the mix. I'll plant it, and we'll see how it does. If it lives, I will consider staying. If it fails, I will probably go."

"That sounds suspiciously like wagering," he said.

"No one wagers with a child's love. No, this is simply a way of saying, 'We'll see.'"

"Good," he answered, "because I have also found out that Lainie and Karl aren't returning, and the land is completely mine now. I have made all the arrangements, including transferring the claim. The house is now mine—or yours. The only thing that Lainie would like is the music box. If you bring that to me, I can send it to them in Wisconsin."

Things were moving quickly, almost too quickly. She needed to get that horse back and ride it home.

She put down her teacup, with the tea completely untasted, and stood. "Is that horrible creature still out there? I should go. I have much to think about."

"I'll get Stonewall for you, and I'll have a few words with him to make him settle down."

"Thank you. Do you mind if I take a peek at my nephew before I leave? It's been so long."

"He's a light sleeper, so be careful," he warned.

He stayed back and let her go to the room by herself. Her face was soft and loving as she pulled a blanket over the boy's legs, which he promptly kicked off again.

He went outside and reached for Stonewall's reins, and the horse flicked his head, trying to move them out of reach, but he was faster. He had everything ready for Mariah when she came out.

"I think this is for the best," he said. "If, after a year, you still think he should be in Massachusetts, perhaps it will be my turn to uproot myself. We will see."

"It's for the boy," she said, nodding. She looked up at him. "Thank you."

Moonlight caught her hair, adding a silver cast to the auburn glow, and her eyes caught the glow of the stars overhead.

There was a time for everything. The Bible even talked about it. And this was the time for him to kiss her.

He touched her cheek, and she lifted her face to him. He lowered his lips—

And the horse nipped his shoulder, ending that moment.

"I told you it was a nasty creature," she said, touching the tip of Ben's nose.

Then she put her foot in the stirrup and was most of the way across the saddle when Stonewall broke the reins free from Ben's grasp, bearing Mariah over the prairie, one foot still under her.

"Bye!" she called as she waved with one free hand. He could see that once again, she was holding to the mane with the other hand. "Pray for us!"

In the span of one evening, his whole life had taken an unexpected turn.

The next afternoon, when he and Jacey were alone, he brought out the drawings the boy had done while traveling with Bo and his family. He was most interested in talking about the one with the rat in the front.

"Can you tell me about this?" he asked the boy.

Jacey ducked his head. "Do I have to?"

"Well, no, I don't suppose you do, but I am curious. What can you tell me about it?"

"It's the building I lived in with my mom in New York City." The sentences began to tumble out. "That's my dad, not you, but my dad in heaven, and those things are his wings." He pointed to the triangles coming out of the head. "My mom is here, and she's laying down because she can't really sit up anymore because she's so sick. And this is Auntie Mariah, except she never did come, although we waited and waited and waited for her. These are snowflakes because it was cold. And these are rats, and I don't want to talk about it anymore."

Ben wrapped the little boy in a deep embrace and whispered to him, "God will always be here for you, and I will always be here for you, and so will your Auntie Mariah."

He would make sure of that.

* * *

The renegade horse put in the barn until Olea or Fred could come get it the next morning, Mariah stood at her front window. The mosquitoes were fierce tonight, so if there was one advantage to having the world's fastest horse as her transportation, it was that not a single insect landed on her during the ride home. In the barn, of course, it had been a different matter, and she scratched her arms and her legs and, oh—this could only happen to her—her mouth.

Today had been like a series of scenes from somebody else's life. She had found her nephew. Or rather, he had found her.

Something had happened in that barn. She hadn't talked to Ben about it, and she might take it to her grave.

She didn't recognize her own nephew, the one she'd come out here for. That was the guilt that dug at her and dug at her and dug at her, but now she was going to have to face it. She had gotten so caught up in earning money to save Lorna and Joshua, that she'd totally forgotten them. Letters were infrequent, visits nonexistent.

It had been her goal to make their lives better, when in fact she could have gone to see them earlier. She could have settled for less money. She hadn't even asked them if they wanted to be saved from the tenement. She suspected they did, but she'd never asked.

Why hadn't she simply gone to New York City and offered her own apartment as temporary and crowded lodging? Why did she decide she had to move them into their own apartment? She'd even chosen it. It was lovely but beyond their means, which meant she'd had to work more, work longer, and delay going to get them.

Her sister had been dead for over five months before she found out.

She was a terrible, terrible sister and aunt, but this option that Ben presented to her gave her the chance to redeem it all.

She opened her little purse and took out the tiny picture she always carried of her and Lorna. Lorna's hair was piled on top of her head in some kind of messy bun that they'd thought was the most fashionable style. She had her arm around Mariah, protectively, and they both grinned widely at the camera.

She remembered the day. They were on top of the world that day, and nothing could ever stop them. They'd stolen away to Coney Island, a place where no reputable woman would go alone, let alone two young women, and stayed only long enough to get it documented on film in a photography cabana. The place terrified them both, and when a man with two teeth and smelling of beer had lurched at them, they had scurried on home.

They found out later they'd managed to end up in the most disreputable part of Coney Island, and there were other parts that were lovely, but they had learned their lesson and never went back again.

She ran her finger over her sister's image. "Lorna, it's time for me to settle down and do what's right."

She paused, and then she said, very softly, "And find out who's right… I—I think he's right."

What was she giving up? He had laid everything out so plainly that she didn't feel as if she had been backed into agreeing to stay for a year. Actually, this had been quite nice, not working six and a half days a week and ten- to twelve-hour days.

He had been about to kiss her until that dim-witted horse had intervened. If she knew how to shoot a rifle, and if she knew where a rifle was—and bullets, of course—she'd actually think about going out and shooting the fiend.

A kiss! Her first kiss, truth be told.

A kiss! He was going to kiss her!

A kiss! And with it an odd little implicit marriage proposal, but she didn't really think he meant it.

Still, a kiss!

And she was now under the lilac year agreement. She knew she'd try her hardest to make the things grow.

Summer ended quickly, and Jacey was back in school. He had to go to Arrow Township's school since there wasn't a school in Prospect. It worked out all right. A parent would take a wagonful of children in the morning, and another picked them up after school. Once the school in Prospect opened, life would be much easier. The plan was to open one school in a year if they could find a qualified teacher and the right facility to house the school.

They'd also agreed to call him Jacey, since that was

the name he'd chosen for himself. He had been told that if he ever wanted to return to *Joshua*, they would be fine with that.

The sewing business had picked up, especially now that Meggin trusted Mariah with the new machine. It put in a line of stitches in record time, and Mariah knew how to keep it in check so it didn't take off like a runaway horse.

Ben tsked anxiously whenever their paths took them past Lars's fields. They were a mess. Plants, partially harvested, hung at awkward angles, almost as if the fields had been completely abandoned. But Lars was still at his house—they had seen him outside, with his characteristic rolling gait—and of course, every day in the mercantile, over at the pickle barrel with the old men.

Ben and Mariah took a trip to Fargo and selected two lilac bushes, prepared for autumn planting. They looked like dead sticks, but the fellow assured them that she could probably expect blooms in the spring.

They planted them that evening, all three of them. "The soil is supposed to be rich in nutrients," Ben said, "and this spot is about as devoid of everything as you can get. So make sure you use your cooking water on them since they'll have extra good things for the bushes. And anything that's left over, you could bury under them, but bury deep, or you'll be operating a hotel for visiting critters."

"You can have all my vegetables," Jacey offered. "Especially that zucchini. Ick."

Ben looked at her and shrugged. "I don't know. He just won't eat it."

She grinned. "Not to make your life harder or anything, but I won't eat it either. What a nasty vegetable. Give me fresh green peas, straight from the pod in the garden! Or beans, pulled right off the fence. Yum."

"You never let me eat right out of the garden," the boy said to Ben. "How come?"

"I don't know," Ben admitted with a smile. "It just never came to that. You can next time."

This was a lovely evening, the three of them together, even if they were planting the lilacs that he was sure would never live. But he knew he'd be paying regular visits to the lilacs, doing everything in his power to keep them alive.

"Jacey has something for you," Ben said and nodded to the boy, who went back to the wagon and brought over a box.

"You can put these on the tree, and it won't look so bare," he said.

He had made paper chains of colored paper, and Mariah helped him loop them around the branches. "There," she said. "Lovely."

"And now," Ben said, "we have another surprise. Everybody in the wagon. We're going to see Olea and Fred."

Jacey and Mariah looked at each other. "Kittens!" they shouted.

When they arrived at Olea and Fred's house, one kitten had already been taken—the gray striped one.

"That's okay," Jacey said. "That means there's one for each of us."

The cats were separated to Jacey's satisfaction. The black one with the white forehead he named Tom and was his cat. The fuzzy one was Abe and became Ben's kitten. The gray and white one was called Victoria and was Mariah's.

They took the kittens home to get them accustomed to their new environments. "This is like Christmas," Jacey said. "But with live presents!"

The kittens played happily together at Ben's house, and after the boy went to bed, Ben and Mariah stayed up for a bit to discuss the day.

"I'm concerned about you staying at that house without any transportation in the winter," Ben said. "It hasn't been an insurmountable problem in the summer, but as we move into snow, I'd feel a lot better if you had some way to get from place to place. What would you think about a little horse and wagon? I saw one in town, and it would be perfect for you."

"Oh, I can't ask you to do that," she said. "You're very kind, but I know that there is an expense associated with that."

"It's not much." He grinned. "It's a very small wagon and a very small horse. And you could pick up Jacey easily. And go back and forth between the houses."

"That sounds like a wonderful idea, and you are so thoughtful to think of it."

He only grinned at her. "Actually it's self-serving.

I'm tired of having to load Jacey in the wagon to take him with us when I bring you home."

"I withdraw the remark about being thoughtful, but I still appreciate the offer of the horse and wagon."

"It'll be in your barn tomorrow," he promised. "But for now, this is one last trek across the prairie with a sleeping boy in the wagon box."

"You know," she said as they traveled the short distance to her house, "I'd always thought of the city as being loud at night. Refuse containers clanked. Fire wagons clanged their bells in alarm. People laughed and shouted, and dogs barked. Where I lived, there was a man who sang opera in Italian every night, not well, but I liked it. But this is absolutely pandemonium. A beautiful pandemonium."

He knew what she meant. The prairie was just as loud but with a different symphony. The night insects buzzed and hummed in a nonstop rhythm. Night birds called to each other loudly. A dog barked—and it could be a township away, sound carried so clearly on the prairie. From somewhere, a locomotive chugged along. A wolf—or perhaps a fox, he didn't know, and he couldn't see at night—bayed plaintively.

When it was cold like this, cold enough to kill off the mosquitoes, a ride on the night prairie was a delight.

Ben stopped the wagon in the middle of the flatness.

"All around us," he whispered in hushed tones of awe, "is the prairie. In a month, you'll hate it. The wind sails right across it and tries to take your skin off your face. The cold will be so relentless you'll wonder who in their right mind would live here. Look around and remember. This is the reason."

Purple and indigo shadows slid across the land, under a starry expanse that stretched from one side of the world to the other.

"It's so beautiful," she murmured. "'He telleth the number of the stars; he calleth them all by their names.' Psalm 147:4. Isn't that the best? To think that he knows how many stars there are, and each one has a name given by Him."

He put his arm around her, and they cozied up under the limitless sky and the cool night air.

"If He knows their names, then He knows ours, too," Ben said.

He turned to look at her. "And He may very well know what this man is about to do to this woman."

Then, finally, after all the waiting, he kissed her.

And the world paused, happy.

First Church knew how to celebrate Christmas, Mariah thought. Every bit of wood that could hold a branch or a swag was decorated with pine or cedar. Candles wrapped in ribbons sat in each window, snuggled in a holder of winter greenery.

"If it can be decorated, it is," Ben said to her as he handed her another white candle to wrap with red ribbon.

"So if I decorate the candle with ribbon, what do I decorate the ribbon with?" she teased.

"Ssh! Don't even mention it. The next thing you know, someone will hand you a box of old fabric ends and ask you to make tiny fans out of each one. And that'll go on the ribbon. And then the fan will need a shiny thing. You get the idea."

"I understand."

So far the experiment was working quite well. She saw Jacey—she still stumbled over the name occasionally—almost every day, and she and Ben had moved into an easy relationship that was clearly leading to love.

The cats were growing fat and obnoxious, constantly underfoot, but worth their weight in the mouse bodies they presented their owners each morning.

For Christmas, Jacey hung new streamers on the bare lilac bushes, adding a bit of color to the now solid-white prairie.

She was coming to terms with their odd little family, and having the three of them together made her very happy.

"I have a gift for you," Ben said as they tucked the last candle up on the altar. "Come with me."

"Shouldn't it wait until Christmas?" she asked. She had made him a new quilted vest, a mélange of the blues from the nighttime prairie. It should make his eyes look extraordinary, but she had kept it tucked away at her house. For Jacey, she'd made an oversized cat that he could sit on in the wagon. Part pillow, part toy, he should like it.

What did he have for her? She followed him to the side room of the church, where the dinner had been held.

"I wanted to give this to you here in the church. It

just seemed right. This was in a box that was sent on from Orphans and Foundlings. It was in the apartment. There wasn't really anything else in it."

"She probably sold it all," Mariah whispered.

"I imagine that's what happened. At the time, it didn't make too much sense, but now it does. Here."

She opened the wrapping and found a photograph of her family: Lorna, her, and their parents. Lorna must have been around seven in it, which would have made her five. The image was still as sharp as the day it was taken.

The frame was new, and she looked at Ben, who nodded. "There wasn't one."

She leaned across and kissed him, very lightly. "This is the kindest, best gift I could have received."

"You are the kindest, best gift I have received," he said.

"Cut the mushy stuff," Jacey said, coming into the side room. "Reverend Timms told me to get you so we could sing some Christmas carols, and then we can all go home. I'm hungry. Let's sing and then go home to eat. And see my cats. And open my presents."

"The Spirit of Christmas has spoken," Ben said with a laugh.

After several rousing choruses of some well-loved Christmas carols, the congregation dispersed, calling greetings to each other across the snow-white prairie.

"I'm glad you brought the cutter," Mariah said to Ben. "It's so romantic."

"And a lot more practical than a wagon in the snow."

Jacey was sitting between them, a buffalo robe over their knees, and as a gentle snow began to fall, she thought nothing could be more perfect.

Chapter 6

Cough. Cough—cough—cough. Cough. Cough.

The sound was relentless, coming from Jacey's bedroom.

Cough. Cough. Cough.

Poor child. He couldn't sleep for all the coughing, and yet the coughing wasn't going to get better without some sleep.

She'd volunteered to stay with her nephew while Ben rode into town in search of help. She'd instructed him to get some menthol, camphor, and eucalyptus oil. Her mother had made a mixture of that, and it had helped relieve chest congestion.

The other alternative was nasty—a concoction of onion and honey—but it also seemed to offer some respite from a cough.

She laid down the needlework she'd brought with her and went back in to look at Jacey. His eyes were sunken, and he was so tired from coughing that he was shaking. At least, though, he didn't have whooping cough. That was a blessing.

This was just a garden variety lung congestion, but it had hit his little body hard.

Both of the cats were cuddled up next to him, probably indicating that his fever had spiked again. She tried to put a cold compress on his face, but he shook it away. "Gives me the shivers," he told her.

She propped him up with extra pillows. "You'll cough less if you're sitting up more," she said to him, and he nodded.

"Would you like me to tell you a story about my cat Victoria?" she asked settling in next to him.

"Yes, please."

"All right. Well, as you might well know, she comes from a fine hunting family. The claws on this particular family are legendary. Some say they're sharper than knives. Others say they're like needles. And still others say they're like tiny pins."

"Abe's are like needles. Tom's are like pins," he explained before breaking into a coughing spasm. She handed him a glass of water to sip from when he had finished.

"Then you know about Miss Victoria Cat's claws. Well, one night, when I was asleep, she decided to go on an expedition."

"Where?"

"I'm not sure," Mariah said slowly, "but I expect it

had to do with a sailing ship. Miss Victoria Cat does like her fish, and where else would she find fish but on the ocean?"

"In the river."

"Perhaps. But Miss Cat dreams big dreams and enjoys grand expeditions, so off she went to find a sailing ship and travel the ocean while I slept."

"Did she find a ship?"

"Oh, that she did. Here's how she did it. She sat in the window, just where she can see the moon across the prairie, and she spied the moon. It was a crescent moon, which, as you might know, is a fishing moon."

"I didn't know that!" he said.

"Nor did I, but Miss Victoria Cat did, and the next thing you know, she had unlatched the window, slid it open, and reached her furry paw across the prairie. And with just one of those extraordinary claws, she snagged the moon. And she got into it and started it swinging back and forth, back and forth, in bigger and bigger arcs until at last it swung her right over the ocean."

"Oh my!" Jacey's eyes were bright. "I can just see her doing that!"

"And there, right in the middle of the ocean, was a fishing boat with a tall mast. She leaped out of the moon and landed on that mast, and her wonderful claws let her climb down the spar and explore the boat. Now most cats do not enjoy being on a boat, but Miss Victoria Cat is a special, daring girl, and she investigated every inch and found enough fish to keep her happy. But then what do you think happened?"

"I don't know," he breathed.

"Well, the sun began to come up, and that meant the moon was going away, so she had to climb back up the mast, leap into the moon again, and let it bring her back to us. I found her this morning at the bottom of my bed, and you know what, Jacey? She smelled just a little bit like fish. Ocean fish. But she isn't telling how that came to be, but I know that it happened just as I told you."

He had finally nodded off to sleep, and she knew he would rest just a short while before coughing again. Maybe by having him sleep sitting up in his bed he could breathe easier.

She shut her eyes and listened to his ragged breathing. *Please,* she prayed, *keep this boy in Your care. I know You do anyway, but I'm just reminding You how important he is to me, to us. You know the names of the stars. The name of this little boy is Jacey.*

The sound of Ben at the front door brought her out of her sleep. She stood quietly and tiptoed to the kitchen, where he had spread out the purchases. "So what do we do?" he asked.

"Mix the stuff up, about equal parts of camphor, menthol, and eucalyptus oil. I'll start preparing the onion and honey."

His face indicated what he thought of that concoction, but as he stirred together the pungent mixture of camphor, menthol, and eucalyptus oil, his eyes began to water, and his nose started to run. "I guess this is about right then, isn't it?"

She laughed. "I guess so. When he wakes up, we'll

smooth it over his chest. It really helps open him up. The onion and honey attacks the congestion. I'm not as convinced about it as I am with the other mixture, but it can't hurt, right?"

"As bad as this smells, he probably won't want to get better," Ben predicted direly.

"Or maybe he'll get better so he can avoid all this. Think positively!"

"Are you going to stay here and administer the poultice?" he asked.

She shook her head. "I have more shirts to do at my house, so I'll just leave you here. It's a nice enough day, I think, and I'll open the curtains and let the sunshine pour on in. It's not quite as good as working outside, but that'll happen again."

The little horse and wagon that he'd bought for her had turned out to be a real blessing. She wasn't using the wagon now because of the snow, but the horse, which Jacey had named Maple Sugar because it was brown and white, managed fine around the drifts.

She'd come back the next day and sit with the boy.

That evening she laid her sewing aside at last and read the Bible. Inspired by Ben, who was almost through Numbers, she was trying to catch up with him.

She read the story of Noah in Genesis and laid the Bible aside to mull over it. What would she do if God told her to build a boat, an ark, especially here in the Dakota Territory? She laughed out loud, startling the cat from its perch on the window. It wouldn't matter where she was. The thought of her building a boat anywhere was ridiculous. Olea couldn't even image that

Mariah could fix a chair with some nails and a hammer, let alone build an ark.

Plus the logistics must have been nightmarish. How did he get the animals to go on board, just two of them? And how did he manage to find food for all of them? And he was six hundred years old.

It was one of her favorite stories, though. God asked Noah to do it, and he did. That simple.

She yawned. It had been a long day, and she scooped up Miss Victoria Cat and took her with her to sleep.

Ben listened to his son's breathing, measuring each inhalation and exhalation, listening for the catch that would signal a coughing spasm.

Praise God. It was good. The crazy concoction that he and Mariah had mixed up had done the trick, and the child was much better.

What they both needed was sleep.

The next day dawned like a January blessing. It wasn't quite the thaw—it was a bit too early for that, Mariah thought, but the air was sweet, and she could almost smell spring behind the morning.

She should probably get over to Ben's house. He had wanted to go to Lars Olsen's house for a while and check in with him, and she could stay with Jacey. She packed a bag with her needlework, and extra thread and pins in case the cats decided to investigate the contents of her pack, and put it by the door.

Miss Victoria Cat was acting very strangely, alternately meowing and hiding. She finally yowled and slipped under the bed, where she emitted a series of high-pitched mournful sounds that set Mariah's teeth on edge.

Was her cat sick?

She dropped to the floor and reached under the bed for the cat, who slithered away and eluded her grasp. Something was not right. Usually the cat was a glutton for attention.

She finally stood up and shrugged. Whatever was bothering the cat was going to have to bother it under the bed. If she couldn't convince it to come out, there was nothing she could do.

Mariah put on her winter coat, buttoned it, pulled on her hat, wrapped a muffler around her neck, and tucked her hands into thick leather mittens she'd found in the house. Her boots were nothing worth bragging about, but they'd do.

She picked up her bag and opened the door. Two steps out, she stopped.

What on earth was that?

She stood motionless, watching what seemed to be the end of the world. A huge white cloud that filled the western sky was rolling toward her, on the ground, and as it came closer, she could hear it, too. It roared, loudly, like a dragon or a locomotive or like God Himself.

Her body wouldn't respond. What was this? She wanted to watch it more, to try to make sense of this anomaly of nature, but she knew at the same time that she really should get back inside the house, away from the windows, with the door latched.

The rumble grew until she finally covered her ears. What was this? A snowstorm tornado?

Suddenly it was upon her.

The snow was unlike any she'd seen before. Tiny and crystalline, almost a snow dust, it drove itself right into her skin and immediately began to crust on her skin. Her left eye, half shut against the wind, began to freeze in that position.

It was so cold, and getting colder.

She struggled against the wind to turn around, and she realized, for the first time, that she might be only a few feet from her door, but unless she moved now and as quickly as she could, she would freeze to death.

This snow dust covered everything, although now she couldn't see six inches past her face. So unusually fine, the snow was thicker than usual.

She finally got to her door, and to get the latch open, she had to take off her gloves. They flew away immediately, and the snow dug into her skin and created a crust over her fingers. She held as tightly as she could to her sewing bag. If it were at all possible to save it, she was going to.

At last, by blocking the wind with her body, she was able to get inside her house. She flung her bag away from the door and tried to wrestle the door shut. The wind fought her at every turn, and the house was getting icier and icier. She had to shut the door or freeze to death.

Finally by pulling on the door and kicking the snow out, she was able to shut the door and latch it. The snow was not going to win.

What was going on? What was this thing? She had seen blizzards certainly in Lowell, but nothing on this scale.

Mariah walked around the little room, feeling the chill on her increase as the winds continued and the temperature dropped. She checked the wood supply by the little metal heating stove. She would be fine if she was cautious.

What *was* this? What *was* this? She kept rubbing her hands, as much from nervous energy as an attempt to unfreeze them. Just that short time without her mittens on made her hands ache and burn. Frostbite.

She reached for the teakettle and got shocked. Touched the stove, got shocked. Tried to light a lamp, got shocked. Even her hair felt like it was moving with the electricity in the air.

This was no normal storm.

She made a cup of tea and watched the storm from inside her house. There was no way anyone could see their way out there. For the first time, she was actually glad that Jacey was sick. That meant he didn't go to school that day, and he wouldn't be out on the prairie in this.

She wrapped her arms around herself. What if he had been out there? What if he had gotten caught in the snow and the wind? He would have died. And Ben, who would have stayed home today with Jacey, was also safe. Just knowing that made it all a bit easier.

The storm rattled the windows as if frustrated that it couldn't get inside. The house wasn't big enough to pace in. She could only take two steps in one direction and two steps in the other. But she took those two steps each way over and over, walking out the rhythm of the wind and snow that beat so incessantly at the walls.

The cat probably still cowered under the bed, and part of her wanted to slide under there with her.

She paced and listened to the storm and prayed for everyone.

At last she got a blanket from her bed and sat in the chair by the stove, until finally she fell mercifully asleep to the sounds of the strange blizzard.

The howl and clamor of the storm finally released its hold in the predawn hours, and Ben walked from window to window, searching the horizon.

He opened the front door and kicked through the accumulated snow. It was astonishingly cold outside, but clear and unclouded. He ran his hand over his face in despair. He had no idea where to even begin.

Probably the best thing was to talk to Mariah first.

He hitched up the cutter to Old Gray, and after making sure that the horse's blanket would offer some protection from the intense cold, they went to her house.

Ben didn't even go to the door to see if she was there before taking Old Gray to her barn. Of course she was there. Only someone who was a complete buffoon would be out on a day like this.

Someone like him.

He got Old Gray warmed up and taken care of, and then he headed to Mariah's house.

Mariah had obviously been sleeping. She was still

groggy as she greeted him, but she quickly regained herself.

"What are you doing here?" she asked. "Where's Jacey? You didn't leave him at home alone, did you?"

He took a deep breath. "Mariah, sit down. This is going to be hard."

"What happened to him?" she asked through gritted teeth. "What happened?"

"I don't know."

"Is he all right?"

"I don't know."

"Then tell me what you do know."

"Yesterday morning, he was much better, and he begged to go to school with the others, and I let him." There, it was out in one long statement.

"Where is he?"

"I don't know. Actually, Lars was the one taking the children to school. He does it fairly regularly since he has a bigger wagon than the others."

"Oh," Mariah said, standing up and facing the window. "This just gets worse and worse. My nephew is gone again, in some kind of crazy Dakota blizzard, and whose care is he in? A man who can't even be bothered to harvest his own fields."

She swiped at the tears that were running down her face.

"If I had to choose a man to entrust my child to," Ben said, "it would be Lars. He may be off-kilter a bit lately, but he's a good man."

"Off-kilter. The man is off-kilter." Mariah shook her head dully. "I cannot believe what I am hearing. Why on earth did you let Jacey go to school? He was sick, and he shouldn't have been outside anyway."

"The morning started out fine, actually better than any other morning this week. You know that. How was I to know what was coming? I'm not even sure what it was. I've never seen anything like it in my entire life. And, just so you know, yes, I have beat myself up every single minute since the storm hit for letting him leave with the others." Ben sank his face into his hands.

"The others. Who are the others? Maybe they know something," she said. She reached for her coat. "Let's go into town and see what we can find out."

A ruckus from outside the house drew her to the window. "As I live and breathe!" she cried. "It's Jacey!"

She opened the door and ran to Lars's wagon. "Jacey!"

Ben was right behind her, and they invited Lars and the other children inside to warm up.

"Just for a moment," Lars said.

"I want to tell the story," Jacey said, "because it happened to me."

"It happened to me, too," another child objected.

"And me. It happened to all of us," a third child piped in.

"Let's hear it from Lars," Ben said. "Then, Jacey, you can tell me again afterward because I know I'll want to hear even more about it."

"We had just started out for the Arrow school when I kind of heard it, kind of felt it. I never seen anything like it, and I think I don't want to ever again, but anyway, I thought right quick whose house we were by, and it turns out that Meggin Sanders's farm is just off the road by where we were."

"Meggin Sanders farms, too. Well, I never!" Mariah breathed.

"Yup, she is a right smart lady. So I pulled the wagon over in that direction, got the horsey moving along, and we sang songs to outrun the blizzard, and the next thing we knew, we were all sitting safe and sound in Meggin's house, having hot chocolate."

"And she has hot chocolate." Mariah shook her head in amazement.

"With whipped cream!" one of the children added.

"Of course. And why not?" Mariah asked.

"So these fine students and I, we weathered out the storm in fine style, didn't we, childrens?" Lars asked them, and the young people chorused a resounding, "Yes!"

Jacey began to wiggle and dance. "Can I tell them? Can I tell them, huh? Can I?"

"You got them ants in your pants," Lars said. "Yeah, sure, go ahead."

"Mr. Olsen and Mrs. Sanders are getting married!"

"Next July. You three going to be there, I hope?" Lars stood. "Time to get these other little ones back to their families. I bet you've got some worried people wondering where you are."

The troupe filed out of the tiny living room, leaving only Ben, Jacey, and Mariah. Victoria, the cat, wandered out and yawned, as if to ask what all the commotion was.

"So, a wedding, huh?" Ben said, absently watching

the cat begin playing with the tassel on Jacey's cap. "That ought to be fun."

He grinned as he realized all the hints that he'd missed about the growing relationship between Lars and Meggin. It explained pretty much everything, including Lars's laughter over his statement that she was going to stay. Ben, of course, thought of Mariah, and Lars thought of Meggin.

He watched as Mariah shot a quick look at Jacey, who was completely involved with the cat, before she leaned close to him and said in a low voice, "The entire deal is canceled. It's over."

And with those short sentences, his world collapsed.

After Ben and Jacey had returned to their house, Mariah looked around the house. In just a short time, she'd managed to make this her own home. Now, she didn't know what to do.

How could she leave her son in a place that had a killer blizzard like this one? She hadn't heard yet, of course, if there were deaths as a result of it, but how could there not be?

And what kind of place had storms like this just spring up, with snow powder and deadly winds and extreme icy temperatures? Maybe, just maybe, was God telling them to go somewhere else where the weather was saner?

It had its own peculiar kind of beauty—she'd come to see that—but when all the tallying was done, Lowell was the place to raise a boy. Not here.

In Lowell, the schools and the houses were next to

each other. Children left school and walked a block or two to their homes. They didn't have to rely on an old man to drive them around the prairie as if they were just field potatoes being dropped off.

It snowed in Lowell, but rarely was it an event worth mentioning in the news. Not like Dakota.

She sat down at her kitchen table with a sheet of paper and a pencil. She figured and refigured and double-checked and triple-checked and finally put the pencil down in desperation. She didn't have enough money to leave with Jacey.

No matter how she cut it, she was going to have to stay longer, at least through April.

She knew she'd have to clarify it with Ben, but she was still so angry that he'd let Jacey leave. The logical part of her mind pointed out that Jacey being sick had nothing to do with the blizzard, and actually, Jacey had seemed remarkably well on their return, a testament to the recuperative power of children.

She was angriest at Dakota itself, with its serene summers and blessed falls. A woman could lose her heart to this land, and then winter would snatch it up and throw it on the ground.

Again, the nagging voice spoke up: *It's easier to be angry at something that can't respond than it is to be angry at yourself, isn't it? If you hadn't made such a series of dreadful, self-centered mistakes back East, you would never have been in this position, and neither would Jacey.*

She put her head on the paper and wept.

* * *

They lived in an icy truce. Ben finally understood why she was unforgivingly upset, but he didn't see any way around it. What had happened had happened. The storm was one of a kind, and the death toll was finally settled at 235. The blizzard covered seven states—he'd never seen a blizzard of that kind, or that magnitude.

But it had happened once, and that was all it took.

January moved into February, and February became March. Spring was tucked behind each breeze that came through, a shy promise of the future.

The people of Prospect put the blizzard behind them as well as they could. They'd been spared any loss of life, but neighboring communities hadn't been so fortunate, and Prospect grieved with its neighbors.

Then the news came from the East Coast. There had been a terrible blizzard there, too. It wasn't the same kind as the one the Midwest had seen. This was a straightforward blizzard, snow and wind and cold.

Ben had come over after Jacey left for school, and he'd found Mariah sitting at the table, a copy of a newspaper in front of her. Her face was ashen.

"Look at this," she said, her finger pointing to an article. "This came tucked inside a shipment that Meggin just received from Boston. There's a newspaper from Boston, and one from Lowell, where I lived, so I took them both to read. Look at this."

"Silence: The wires all down." He read the headline out loud. "Oh my gosh. The city is absolutely stopped dead by the storm. No travel in or out of the city."

"And here's Lowell's." She handed him the second

newspaper, where he read about the thick snowfall that had brought that city to a halt, too.

He scanned it quickly. "They turned off the electricity, and the telegraph wires are down. That's amazing."

She leaned back and studied him. "I don't know what to say," she began. "I feel like I should spend my entire life apologizing. And I want to start with you."

He started to object, but she waved his words away. "No. I am sorry. I've just made a mess of things for a long time, and it's about time I confessed and asked for everyone's forgiveness."

"Mariah, come here." He opened his arms, and she came into the embrace as naturally as if she were born to it. "What's wrong?"

"I started off badly in Lowell." She sniffled against his shoulder. "I was playing the role of Lady Bountiful. I planned that I would come into my sister's life and whisk her and her son away from those dreadful tenements, and life would be better because of me, me, me. I had my role in their lives already laid out. I was to be their savior, but they didn't necessarily want that."

"They wanted you," he said softly, thinking of the drawing Jacey had done in St. Paul.

"I would like to think that. But it didn't occur to me. Ever. I was so virtuous, working long hours at two jobs, preparing, always preparing for The Event, when I would save them."

"Your intentions were good," he offered, trying to mollify the situation.

"No, they weren't. They were dreadful. If I'd truly wanted to make their lives better, I would have gone to visit them, found them affordable housing, perhaps had them move in with me." She remained silent for a moment.

"Do you know what the worst part of all this is?" she finally asked.

He smoothed the back of her hair. "What?"

"You knew about my sister's death before I did."

"How could that be?" he asked.

She pulled away from him and walked into the living room. "It's true. You knew from the minute you saw Jacey. January, right? I knew when I went to make my grandiose gesture of freeing them—in June. This is how devoted a sister I am, Ben. She was dead, and I didn't know it. And I don't know where she's buried, either."

"Oh, my dear." He had no idea what to say.

"So it's my fault that Jacey had to go onto the Orphan Train, although he did find a good home with you, I acknowledge that. But if I had been there as I should have been, none of this would have happened."

"Mariah, life is full of missteps and things we should have done. Do not rip yourself apart over this."

She shook her head. "And then when he came tearing into the barn to see the kittens, I—" Her voice broke, and she finished in a whisper. "I didn't recognize him. It had been too long since I'd seen him last. He recognized me, but I didn't recognize him."

He thought of the absolute sadness in the boy's voice when he'd told Ben that he and his mother had waited for Mariah to come, and she hadn't. He decided that he wouldn't share that story with her or with anyone else. It was Jacey's privilege to decide on that, and he felt that the boy would probably never speak of it again.

"Mariah," he said, "there's one way to make sure that the boy has everything he needs. He'll never be hungry, never sleep in a tenement, never worry about who might love him because he'll have all the love a boy can consume."

"Sure," she said. "He can live with you."

"He can live with *us*."

"Us?"

He cupped her face in his hands. "I love you, Mariah Rose. I have since the moment you stepped off the train and I saw you for the first time. I love you with all your beauty and, yes, with all your flaws. You have the best heart and the kindest soul I can imagine. Mariah, will you marry me?"

Mariah stared into his eyes and saw her future. Dakota, and Joshua, and love. Happiness. Contentment.

She could stop fighting herself, stop torturing herself for what she hadn't done. Instead, she could do what she should have done a long time ago.

Admit the truth.

This moment's truth was that she loved Ben. She trusted him. She needed him.

She could never leave him, and she could never leave Dakota. They were parts of her heart, and if her heart had been empty before, it was only because it had been saving a spot for this man and this place.

It was time to stop grieving. The night before she'd read in her Bible a passage from the Psalms. "He that goeth forth and weepeth, bearing precious seed, shall doubtless come again with rejoicing, bringing his sheaves with him."

It was time to end the weeping, time to rejoice…in this fertile land called Dakota.

She nodded. "Yes. Absolutely, positively, completely yes! But I want to show you something."

She led him to the front door of her house. "Look at these little overachievers," she said, pointing to the twin lilac bushes. "It's only mid-March, and they're already greening up, and I wouldn't be surprised to see them bloom first."

He smiled as he pulled her into his arms for one more kiss. "It's going to take more than a monstrous blizzard to stop us, isn't it?"

She only replied, "Mmmmmm."

Epilogue

"The church smells divine," Olea whispered and then giggled. "I guess that's the best way for a church to smell, isn't it?"

The entire sanctuary was decorated with tufts of lilacs. Olea's dress was in the same delicate shade of purple. Mariah's gown was a creamy white with a lavender velvet drape, and she carried a bouquet of the sweetest lilacs she could find—and they'd been right at her front door.

There had been one thing that bothered her. She had no family, except for Jacey, who waited at the front of the church with Ben. She had walked Lorna down the aisle at her wedding, and the two sisters had planned for Lorna to do the same when Mariah got married.

But Lorna was gone.

This was the happiest day of her life, and yet she felt so alone.

She'd confided to Ben her concern about not having any relatives to walk her down the aisle, but Ben had told her not to worry. All would be fine.

It was easy for him to say. His sister was here. Maybe she would walk with her.

Mariah turned to ask her, but Olea shook her head as the wedding march began.

"Go!" Olea whispered. "Now!"

Mariah began the lonely walk down the aisle, blinking back tears as she saw Ben smiling at her.

She was just being silly. He was all that mattered. In a few minutes, in front of God and the gathered guests, they would declare their love and become husband and wife.

There was a growing sound around her, and she realized that everyone was leaving their seats, row by row, and joining her, walking beside her and behind her, all around her, toward the altar. She looked at Olea, who had tears in her eyes. "We're all your family," she said. "We're all walking with you."

At the front were Jacey and Fred and, of course, Ben.

She was surrounded with love on this prairie. She couldn't imagine a better place to be and maybe, even, to raise more children.

The wedding was over entirely too quickly. She wasn't sure what she'd promised to do, but she was sure it was nothing out of the ordinary because no one had gasped.

"I would like to present to you Mr. and Mrs. Benjamin Harris," Reverend Timms announced.

The congregation applauded, and soon Mariah stepped out of the sanctuary a changed woman. "My husband," she said softly as she and Ben embraced.

"My wife," Ben responded.

"And me, too," said Jacey, hugging their knees.

* * * * *

Historical note

The Schoolhouse Blizzard is also called the School-children's Blizzard or just the Children's Blizzard, and it occurred January 12–13, 1888. It is so named because of the high death toll of children who were caught in it while attempting to leave school.

The East Coast had a blizzard on March 12 of the same year, which devastated utilities, transportation, and housing, and took approximately a week to dig out from.

REQUEST YOUR FREE BOOKS!

2 FREE CHRISTIAN NOVELS
PLUS 2
FREE
MYSTERY GIFTS

HEARTSONG
PRESENTS

YES! Please send me 2 Free Heartsong Presents novels and my 2 FREE mystery gifts (gifts are worth about $10). After receiving them, if I don't wish to receive any more books I can return the shipping statement marked "cancel." If I don't cancel, I will receive 4 brand-new novels every month and be billed just $4.24 per book. That's a savings of 20% off the cover price. It's quite a bargain! Shipping and handling is just 50¢ per book in the U.S.* I understand that accepting the 2 free books and gifts places me under no obligation to buy anything. I can always return a shipment and cancel at any time. Even if I never buy another book, the two free books and gifts are mine to keep forever.

159 HDN FT97

Name
(PLEASE PRINT)

Address
Apt. #

City   State   Zip

Signature (if under 18, a parent or guardian must sign)

Mail to the **Reader Service:**
IN U.S.A.: P.O. Box 1867, Buffalo, NY 14240-1867

Not valid for current subscribers to Heartsong Presents books.

* Terms and prices subject to change without notice. Prices do not include applicable taxes. Sales tax applicable in N.Y. This offer is limited to one order per household. All orders subject to credit approval. Credit or debit balances in a customer's account(s) may be offset by any other outstanding balance owed by or to the customer. Please allow 4 to 6 weeks for delivery. Offer available while quantities last. Offer valid only in the U.S.

Your Privacy—The Reader Service is committed to protecting your privacy. Our Privacy Policy is available online at www.ReaderService.com or upon request from the Reader Service.

We make a portion of our mailing list available to reputable third parties that offer products we believe may interest you. If you prefer that we not exchange your name with third parties, or if you wish to clarify or modify your communication preferences, please visit us at www.ReaderService.com/consumerschoice or write to us at Reader Service Preference Service, P.O. Box 9062, Buffalo, NY 14269. Include your complete name and address.

REQUEST YOUR FREE BOOKS!

2 FREE INSPIRATIONAL NOVELS
PLUS 2
FREE
MYSTERY GIFTS

Love Inspired

ReaderService.com

Manage your account online!

- Review your order history
- Manage your payments
- Update your address

> ### We've designed the Reader Service website just for you.

Enjoy all the features!

- Reader excerpts from any series
- Respond to mailings and special monthly offers
- Discover new series available to you
- Browse the Bonus Bucks catalogue
- Share your feedback

Visit us at:
ReaderService.com